EMPTY POCKETS

EMPTY POCKETS

NEW AND SELECTED STORIES

DALE HERD

COFFEE HOUSE PRESS

MINNEAPOLIS · 2015

Coffee House Press books are available to the trade through our primary distributor, Consortium Book Sales & Distribution, cbsd.com or (800) 283-3572. For personal orders, catalogs, or other information, write to: info@coffeehousepress.org. Coffee House Press is a nonprofit literary publishing house. Support from private foundations, corporate giving programs, government programs, and generous individuals helps make the publication of our books possible. We gratefully acknowledge their support in detail in the back of this book. Visit us at coffeehousepress.org.

LIBRARY OF CONGRESS CIP INFORMATION

Herd, Dale, 1940–
[Short stories. Selections]
Empty pockets : new and selected stories / by Dale Herd.
pages cm
ISBN 978-1-56689-377-0 (pbk.) — ISBN 978-1-56689-382-4 (ebook)
I. Title.
PS3558.E66A6 2014
813'.54—DC23
2014006996

PRINTED IN THE UNITED STATES

FIRST EDITION | FIRST PRINTING

ACKNOWLEDGMENTS AND PERMISSIONS

The author is indebted to the following publishers for permission to reprint copyrighted work: Donald Allen, Four Seasons Foundation, for *Early Morning Wind;* Lee Robert De Lapp, Richard Gates, and Terry Nemeth, Mudra, for *Diamonds;* and Michael Wolfe, Tombouctou Books, for *Wild Cherries.*

The author would also like to thank the following poets for their support in bringing this book into existence: Bill Berkson, Michael Lally, Lewis MacAdams, Duncan McNaughton, Kevin Opstedal, and Michael Wolfe.

This book is for
Deborah Beatriz Blum

from
EARLY MORNING WIND (1972)

from
DIAMONDS (1976)

from
WILD CHERRIES (1980)

EMPTY POCKETS
AND OTHER STORIES

from

EARLY MORNING WIND

(1972)

Eric

She had a kid asleep in the bedroom. I asked her if she wanted to ball and she said yes. She got her gun six times. I told her I was selling my car and all my belongings and buying a sailboat and sailing to Australia. I said she could go but she'd have to pay. How much she said. A dollar thirty-seven I said. She said not bad. Then she said how much for Eric. I said ten thousand dollars.

Seduction and Cuckoldry

Frank and Geno were new friends. Frank had just started in the office and Geno began taking him to lunch. They would eat in the University District to watch the girls walking to and from school. Watching the girls was much more fun than was eating, but each watched for a different reason.

Frank was newly married and he was shy about his wife. When he was alone with her he found it hard to approach her. Looking at other girls excited him, and if he became excited enough he could go home and forget his shyness. He felt guilty about it, but it worked.

Geno, however, had been married for five years and shyness was not his problem. He was seriously thinking of leaving his wife, and looking at new lovely girls encouraged his desire for freedom.

After a few lunch hours together, Geno began telling Frank some of his personal problems, problems that Frank didn't like.

Geno admitted to playing around. And while it made him seem wild and free, things Frank believed a man should be, he distrusted Geno for it and was more than a little frightened by him.

On their fourth noon hour together, Frank and Geno were inside a sandwich shop watching the girls walking by. It was a bright spring day and they were talking about getting free of their jobs.

Both agreed that life was too short to work for someone else. Geno said quitting might be the final straw for Julie. Frank said his worry was the other way around.

"If I quit, Betty might leave me."

"Good," Geno said. "Why not?"

"What do you mean?" Frank laughed.

"You'll be free then," Geno said.

"Sure," Frank said, yet he felt threatened. Recently there had been times when he found himself wondering if Betty ever thought sexually about Geno.

"I don't want other women," Frank said.

"Maybe not," Geno said. "You never know."

"I don't," Frank emphasized. "Why do you?"

"I really don't know what I want."

"Maybe you're just looking for an escape."

"Maybe," Geno smiled. "It is funny, though. I never like the girls I get."

"Really?" Frank said.

"They either kiss wrong or smell bad or something is wrong with them. I'll say that for Julie: she's certainly a clean girl."

Frank laughed.

"But the real thing is," Geno said, "is that I feel bad afterward and I start acting good to Julie and she responds and things go nicely for a time."

"I see," Frank said, sitting back. He had been listening intently. Two nights before he and Betty had eaten out with Geno and Julie for the first time. They had just met Julie, and while they were waiting for the meal Geno said, "Do you know what Julie was doing when I came home? She was talking to herself in the mirror." Betty had laughed sympathetically, saying she often did the same thing. But Julie had flared, saying, "Do you know what Geno does? He poops in his shorts!" Frank had been startled. He had looked at Geno. Geno hadn't flinched. Geno gently explained that Julie had been rehearsing for a speech class. But Julie stayed angry throughout the meal. Talking afterward Frank and Betty agreed the outburst was unbelievable. Frank said he had been very impressed with Geno's calm. Betty said, "I don't see how they got married." But now, Frank felt, Geno's calm wasn't impressive. It was based on deception. He saw that Julie wasn't entirely to blame.

"Your wife seems nice," Geno said. "You've got a good thing there."

"Thank you," Frank said.

"I'd like to start a new thing," said Geno. "I really would. I guess the only thing to do is break up. These other women aren't the thing. The real thing is my guilt. I get to feeling so bad I can't even function. I mean, after a while I get so bad I can't even make it with anybody!"

"No kidding!" Frank said. "Does Julie know you play around?"

"God, no!" Geno said. "Never arm a woman! But never!"

"No?"

"No!"

"Why not?" asked Frank.

"Because they'll use it against you," Geno said. "Just like the other night when Julie came out with that shorts and shit thing."

"Really," Frank said, sitting back again. He was amazed.

"I could have killed her," Geno said.

"Really," Frank repeated, talking almost to himself. "Are you going to leave her?"

"Maybe," Geno said. "I don't know."

"Well," Frank said, "if you need a place to stay you can always put up at our place. We have an extra bed."

"Good," Geno said. "Fine."

The rest of the lunch hour Frank paid no attention to the girls. He thought only about how Geno really was inside. He could hardly wait to tell Betty. Men were nothing inside, he thought. They were just like babies. Frank was more excited than if he had been looking at the girls.

Geno, however, did look at the girls. And the more he looked, the more he began thinking about Betty. She was really nice, he thought, but hell, Frank was his friend.

Twins

Jenny, her body still heavy and swollen, was sitting with Beth at the kitchen table. Down the hall in the living room I could see the two pink bassinets.

"I'm not kidding," Jenny was saying, "her mind is just going wacky since I've had the twins. She's making me so damn nervous . . ."

"Take it easy," Beth said.

"Who?" I asked.

"Grandma," Beth said.

"Do you know what she did yesterday?" said Jenny. "She sat in the living room and cried because Hill didn't say hello to her and she thought that meant no one wanted her here. Mother had to give her an alcohol rub and put her to bed like a baby. She's Mother's baby now. Isn't that funny?"

"It's her age," Beth said. "Her arteries are hardening."

"No," Jenny said, "it's simply attention. Since the twins came, she's simply not getting enough attention. She makes me so damn mad! She hasn't even once asked to hold them! Not once!"

"I think I'll go take a look," I said.

I went down the hall into the living room. The babies were asleep, one on its stomach, its tiny fists clenched, the other on its back, its little eyes wrinkled like an old woman's.

As I came back in the kitchen, Jenny wanted to know what I thought.

"They're perfect," I said. "You're a lovely girl."

She smiled and brushed the hair back off her face. Beth gave me a wink.

Happy Dreams

About a week before Celia called, saying, "Well, we did it. I finally feel like a woman again . . ."

Leaning over, a good lovely look on his face, telling us this shortly after visiting Celia and Gene for his first look at the new babies, Willy said, "Christ, seeing her nurse those twins really did it to me. The first time I ever saw anyone nurse, it was twins. I was settling a route dispute in this guy's house, having a beer in the kitchen, and the guy's wife came in, sat down, lifted out her breasts, and started nursing two babies just like that. My God, I wanted to knock them off and plunge in there myself. Seeing Celia do the same thing was just a bit too much. Beautiful women should know better."

We laughed. Right after that, Willy left to visit his girl and Gerri called and told Celia the story. Celia laughed and said, "Yes, but did he like the babies?" Gerri laughed and said, "He didn't say, but doesn't that turn you on? How long has it been? It's been more than three months now, hasn't it? Hasn't Gene complained?" "Oh, no," Celia answered. "You know Gene."

Then, three days later, Celia called, using merrily those special sister to sister tones, not talking about her babies, saying this to Gerri: "My God, Ger, the dream I had! I don't believe it! Promise you won't tell? Ever? It's about Willy. Yes! Remember what you told me? God! Yes! We were all sitting at the table, you, me, Phil, Gene. I was feeding the twins, watching you guys play bridge, and Willy was under the table. Yes! No! No one knew. And all I had on was a housecoat! No! Nothing else! And he started kissing my legs! Yes! No! Yes, I did like it, but I couldn't keep my face still! I was scared to death Gene would look up and see my face and Willy kept kissing higher and higher . . . it was simply . . . no . . . ha ha ha . . ."

Ripped

The Cedars was a downhome, funky bar—Swan, Moody, Mick the Hillbilly, Dead Ed, Donna. Going back was always great. It was out in Ballard, out in the old industrial section with train tracks crossing the streets, concrete underpasses, past wrecking yards, junkshops, old hotels for old men. We were always stoned en route, and the twenty-minute ride from the U District could take light-years but was always all right. Swan would take things down into the crowd; he didn't dig the leader-of-the-band trip, so he would jump down off the stage out of the colors and ask everyone to shout or stomp or move. First you were moving and then sweating and things would start mixing in and mixing out and going on the same, hands, hair, hips, feet, up on the stage into the lights there cupping the harp to the mike, you could really lay it out, putting it all into pulling it straight out from under you, feeling yourself pulling the power from the floor, the concrete, the ground, the earth, all of it coming up and out into everybody, into everywhere, Swan laying it on with you, Moody the same, Moody constant, always happy, you happy sweating, everyone happy, everyone going on in everybody, and so it would go, anyone could get up there, most of us did, but the place was always empty of regular customers, the management didn't dig Swan's band, so when he'd do something similar, anything, play with his teeth, or let "American Man" run on out the full set, never giving the dancers a break, they'd threaten to can the whole group, they wanted a straight country-western shitkicking beer outfit in there, but they weren't making enough money to pay for it, so they were stuck with Swan. The place was nearly always empty until we got there, all our own crowd, all us stoners, dropouts, longhairs, fuckups, dope fiends, all of us all getting it on, it was always a hell of a good time, no one ever got busted, some of us even got laid out there, picking up some of the local stuff, Buc, in particular, Buc had a great time with two of the local hogs, two peroxide-tipped bangers that wanted his body, so he took them on outside in Moody's Chevrolet, everyone walked outside and looked at the steamed-over windows.

Captain Baa Baa

When the first contingent of American troops withdrawn from Vietnam comes home in the summer of '69 at McChord Air Force Base, General Richard C. Williamson, former Commander in Chief in Vietnam and then current Army Chief of Staff, is there to greet two-ninths of them with a handshake.

For many of these men (all sharp looking, all deeply tanned, all wearing highly polished combat boots and clean combat fatigues, sleeves rolled to the bicep), certainly for those who wear a small round button in their lapel that reads We Try Harder, the slogan of Avis Rent A Car, America's second leading car rental agency, the greeting by Williamson, the highest-ranking officer they have ever seen, is particularly memorable.

Standing tall, every inch the picture of the nation's top general, wearing no extra insignia save the gold and silver braid on the glossy brim of his high-crowned hat, the four silver stars on each collar of his summer dress blouse, and a single blue infantryman's badge over his left breast pocket, Williamson's firm grip, six-foot-one-inch height, and rugged face of hard jawline, lean cheeks, and massive black eyebrows accent his position of command and lend power to the solemnity of the occasion.

And when giving the last address of the afternoon to the entire contingent of 814 men, the sun hammering at his face, occasionally ricocheting off his stars, but never affecting his eyes, eyes protected by shadow cast from the brim of his hat, his bearing, to every man there, reinforces the words he speaks:

"I want to convey to you the appreciation of our nation—appreciation for a job well done.

"You have grown and developed while you have been in uniform. You will find yourself more mature, more dedicated to the service of others, more responsible, more realistic, and more practical than your contemporaries who have not served.

"You have served while others stood by, and talked, and demonstrated.

"But, of course, you have demonstrated too.

"You have demonstrated your responsibility by doing your duty for your country.

"Those who stay in the Army will benefit from your experience in Vietnam."

Earlier in the day, shortly before the contingent lands in the nine silver C-141 transports, Williamson presides over another ceremony. Hatless this time but, as later, not seeming to look anywhere but straight ahead, surrounded by aides, base officers, their aides, doctors, military and civilian newsmen and photographers, Williamson walks through the wards of Madigan General Hospital and decorates six of the wounded already home from Vietnam.

For five of the men, all enlisted men, the hospital staff has made the normal frantic pre-inspection preparation: clean bedding put on all beds; walls, windows, woodwork, and floors washed; all tables, chairs, food trays, crash carts, bedpans and urinals, books, magazines, newspapers, and personal effects hidden away under beds and shoved into closets; each man given his personal uniform, cleaned and pressed, complete with rank and insignia.

The sixth man, a twenty-five-year-old Captain, presented presents a special problem. Struck by a Viet Cong mortar fragment, he now has a two-inch-long indentation on the top left side of his shaved skull and a steel plate beneath the indentation. Since his vocabulary is limited to one word, the word baa, and since he is neither able to eat nor dress nor get out of bed by himself, the ward attendants have to feed, shave, have his bowels move, and dress the Captain, as well as satisfy what other wants he might have, all at the proper time just before Williamson arrives, to prevent a possible breakdown in either his appearance or behavior.

The Captain, apparently upset, utters long and loud baas

throughout his preparations. His father, a rancher from Nevada, stands on the right side of the bed attempting to calm him down as the attendants finish. He offers the Captain the urinal, to crank down the bed, to place him in the new electrically propelled wicker wheelchair on the left side of the bed. Each suggestion meets only with louder baas and agitated waves of the Captain's hands. His father is asking him if he wants a hypo when Williamson and the entourage enter the ward.

Immediately the Captain stops baaing.

Williamson, looking neither left nor right, strides rapidly forward. The Captain remains quiet. Williamson reaches the bed. Everyone stops. An aide steps forward and begins reading the citation. Williamson steps up to the Captain, stopping before the wheelchair. He pins a Bronze Star, then a Purple Heart over the Captain's left breast pocket. Six flashbulbs explode. He shakes the Captain's hand. The aide finishes reading. Williamson reaches across the bed and shakes hands with the father. Tears appear in the Captain's eyes.

Then Williamson salutes and moves away, the entourage following. The Captain jerks forward, then back, watching them go out along the row of beds. His right hand half rises to his forehead, then falls, and he begins baaing again, louder and louder, each baa gaining in speed and pitch over the one before.

Old Hotels

His wife left him in 1950 and he never got over it. He cooked at the hotel where I bellhopped, and every time he got paid he'd go out and buy T-bones and cook two and give me one. He drank all the time, and every time he got drunk he'd say the same things over and over. "Let's see if you can name all the teams in the Big Ten. Let's see if I can do it. I can do it." He never did. He'd always leave one out. He'd say, "Did I say Ohio, the Ohio State Buckeyes? Did I?"

He had bad congestion and coughed all the time. The drinking made it worse. He drank beer in the head and after his shift he'd be drunk and want me to go with him in the elevator. The motion of the elevator made him sick and phlegm would dribble out his mouth. Then he'd want me to go to his room. He didn't like being alone there. Every time I'd go up with him in the elevator I'd end up putting him to bed, clothes and all. No matter which way you laid him, faceup or facedown, he'd put his hands on his crotch and start hunching. If I started to leave he'd begin to cry. I'd have to sit with him until he fell asleep.

The Normal Girl

They married in hometown Minnesota when she was nineteen. The marriage lasted eight years. During that time he tried a variety of occupations. He worked in a gas station. He painted window signs. He spent three years at college as a painting student and sold kitchenware door-to-door. He did layout for a newspaper, went on unemployment, and painted on his own through one winter and spring. He clerked in a liquor store. He tended bar. He drove a taxicab. She went where he went, lived where he wanted to live. Four days after her twenty-sixth birthday, sitting in their apartment overlooking a swimming pool in Santa Barbara, California, she told him she wanted a normal life.

"What's that mean?" he asked.

"It means I'm a normal girl raised by normal parents and I want a home and I want a baby."

"Sure you do," he said. "Who doesn't? I do too. I want a baby by you. I've always wanted a baby by you."

"No," she said, "that's not what I mean. Don't you want a child of your own?"

"Not especially."

"Well, I do," she said. "I want us to get a home and you a full-time job and I want a baby."

"I'd like to have a child."

"And a washing machine. I'm not having a baby unless we have a washing machine.

"I really mean it," she said.

"I believe you. Just don't push and maybe it will happen. I'd like it to happen. I really would."

"I mean it, Douglas.

"And I am thinking of us," she said, "for both of us. Either we make it together or we don't. I want a child."

"I understand."

She left off the conversation and went into the kitchen. She knew not to argue. That only brought rage from him. She would wait and see.

The next morning Douglas got up without saying anything, fixed his own breakfast, and left for work without saying goodbye. When he came home in the afternoon, he wasn't talking.

She left him alone.

During dinner he said he had some heavy ideas that needed working out, really strong ideas that would push de Kooning to the wall, maybe, maybe.

He got up from the table, went into the living room, started putting newspaper on the floor. Then he tacked up four huge sheets of clean butcher paper on the wall.

She went in and watched. It was the first painting he had done in some months. He worked fast and athletically, a cigarette in his mouth, attacking the paper in long black smears.

She went to bed and read.

Around midnight he got in bed and wanted to have her.

"No," she said.

"What's the matter?"

"Nothing."

"Yes, there is."

"You already know."

"Damn it," he said.

"Just don't touch me."

"You really mean it, don't you?"

"Yes."

"Listen, Gwen, consider me in this. I don't know enough yet. I haven't experienced enough yet."

"Having a family isn't dying."

"I don't think so either."

"Then do something, for God's sake."

"That's easy to say."

"You make me sick," she said. "You're so goddamned selfish I can't believe it."

"You're not making sense."

"Oh, yes I am. I completely am."

"Listen, hon, listen. Give me one more chance. I've got something going out there. I know it. Really. What I want us to do is move to L.A. That's where the big art dealers are. It's not New York anymore, it's L.A. All you have to do is get to know one and doors open. It's as simple as that."

"Okay," she said. "Go."

"I want us to go."

"No," she said. "This is it. I've moved enough."

"You don't think I can paint."

"No," she answered. "I'm not thinking about you."

"Who the hell is selfish? I mean, you've had your belly filled for the last six years. Where the hell did that come from?"

"You should go," she said.

"Fuck you," he sprang out of bed. "I will!"

"You know, Douglas, I really mean it."

"So do I!"

She rolled over and turned on the light. He was standing within arm's length, looking straight at her. She got out on the other side and went to the closet, reaching up for his suitcase on the top shelf.

"What are you doing?"

She tossed the suitcase on the bed and stood looking at him, leaning forward, feeling herself losing control.

"Go!" she said, "Go! Go! Go! You asshole! You crybaby!"

"I will!" he shouted.

She rushed to the bathroom and slammed the door.

He left about twenty minutes later, apparently taking most of his things. His big trunk was gone and all the rolled-up papers of new paintings. She imagined she could hear the car still going away up the street, and she began to feel that something inside her was really and finally broken and a sick, shaky feeling came over her. She could hear a car going away. She walked out of the living room where she had been standing by the darkened window and returned to bed. It was totally quiet in the room and she lay facedown, waiting for the feeling to pass.

In the morning when she awoke, Douglas wasn't there. She sat down at the kitchen table and wrote home, asking her parents what to do. Then she telephoned home. "Come here," was her mother's reply. "If he won't take responsibility, let him go. There are plenty of others who will."

"I don't think he's going to return, Mama."

"Come home then. I'll send you the money."

"I think I should wait. I don't like the feelings I have. I do love him."

"Whatever you think is best, darling, but don't stay alone. Women aren't meant to live alone. You'd be better off here. If he wants you he can get you here as well as there. You owe us a visit anyhow. I'll send you the money. Take the train. A nice train ride will be good for you."

"Thank you, Mama, maybe I will. I want to wait awhile though. I don't want to be impulsive anymore."

"Okay, darling. I'm sending the money this afternoon."

The money came the next morning, a cashier's check for five hundred dollars, enough money to pay the rent, buy some new clothes, and travel well. She felt momentarily joyful when she saw the amount. It was more money than she had ever seen at one time.

Two days passed without word from Douglas. Gwen spent the time packing her clothes and boxing up their possessions. She didn't expect him to call. She hoped he wouldn't until after she was gone. She wanted him to worry.

When he did call it was what she had expected. He wasn't in L.A., he was in San Francisco, could she come? He was god-awful sorry, he wanted her to come, he had located a nice apartment with a view, she would like the city, it was a beautiful city. Her answer was one more week, if he didn't return by then she was going back home to Minnesota, she already had the ticket. He hung up.

The week passed and he didn't return. She took the Santa Fe Chief out of Los Angeles back to Minneapolis but home was a disaster. Once there all the reasons that compelled her to marry years ago returned. Her mother was still patronizing and full of complaints. Her father was distant and unwarm. The town was totally unchanged and dull. Her old girlfriends who had married and stayed were dull and married to boring men. Getting drunk on weekends wasn't her idea of fun. Despite a vow not to, she wrote Douglas and closed by saying she missed him. No reply came and after writing a second letter with the same result she called long distance hoping he would have a telephone. He did, it was a San Francisco number, when he answered, almost before she knew what she was saying, she blurted out how sorry she was.

"I want to join you," she said.

"I don't have any money," he said. "We'll have to wait."

"I have some. Dad will give us some."

"No," Douglas said, "I don't want any obligations to them."

"You don't want me to come."

"No," he said, "just wait."

"Is there someone else?"

"No, not at all."

"Swear to God?"

"Swear," he said. "Just take it easy. I'll send the money as soon as I can."

"Promise?"

"Promise."

"Okay," she said. "I love you. I know that sounds stupid, but I do."

"I love you too."

"Write me."

"I will."

"I can't hang up."

"I know," he said.

But he didn't write for one good reason. He had a new girl, a deeply involving girl. Gwen didn't know this, but she knew what he had done in the past, and as the days passed without any mail she slowly became frantic and began a series of phone calls usually placed late at night after her parents were asleep. Each time Douglas answered he would deny there was someone else. Gwen would end up crying, telling him she was lonely, desperately lonely. On those occasions when there was no answer, she imagined him making love to someone else, fantasies that gradually began to absorb all her attention.

Her mother suggested a psychiatrist and Gwen agreed. The doctor was gentle with her, listened to her story, made no judgments, told her it was not unusual, gave her some tranquilizers, and suggested, if she could, that it might be best to forget Douglas, take what was valuable from the experience, and think of new ways, possibly, to live.

"It's a matter of values," he said. "Douglas is still looking for himself. You're not. May I suggest something further? Start school, for instance? We have a good community college here. You're a very bright girl. You'd do well."

"No," Gwen said, "I hate it here. I never really understood that, but it's true. I don't belong in this life."

"What do you mean?"

"I belong somewhere else. Out on the coast. If not with Douglas at least with someone like him. Not entirely like him. Someone grown up but someone who isn't boring, who isn't dead inside. Sometimes I'm afraid I'm becoming dead inside and I get scared, really scared."

"I see," the doctor said.

At home Gwen told her parents she wanted to return to the coast, to go to San Francisco. Surprisingly, her father gave her a hug, told her he had always liked Douglas, and wrote her out a check for three hundred dollars.

"My blessings, sweetheart," he said.

Later that day when her father had left the house, her mother tried to talk her out of it, but Gwen wouldn't listen.

Four days later she arrived in San Francisco and checked into the YWCA. For a moment, standing in the lobby, she debated whether to call first or to freshen up and pay a surprise visit. A slight edge of fear decided her to call.

Douglas was home. She said she hadn't meant to startle him, wasn't trying to spy on him, yes, she was in the city. She hoped he wanted to see her, she had changed, she was willing to live on his terms, willing to live free, she would even work while he painted, she did believe in his work, was he painting, could she come to wherever he was?

"As a matter of fact," he said, "I was just going downtown when you called. I'll be right down, say twenty minutes."

"Oh, good," she said.

"But I better warn you," he said. "I don't want you to misunderstand. I've already filed for divorce."

"No," she said.

"I'm sorry, Gwen, it's true. The papers have already been sent out to you."

"What's that mean?"

"It means I want a divorce."

"No!"

"I'm sorry, but it's true."

"You don't mean it."

"I do."

"My God," she said.

"Listen," he said, "be calm. I'm really glad you're here. Really. Now don't go away. I'll be right down. I really do want to talk to you."

She listened to him hang up the phone and she held on to the receiver. She waited for the buzzing to stop and then realized she was crying, her mouth actually fluttering. She pulled open the door of the booth and went out, not hanging up the phone. She went back and hung it up. She walked over to a couch by the far wall and sat down.

That son of a bitch, she thought, he's not going to do this to me. He can't. I won't let him.

She got up and walked over to the ladies' room. Going inside she caught a glimpse of herself crying in the long mirror above the washbasins. She watched the door shut behind her, then bent over, washed her hands, then her face, taking off all the makeup. She looked at herself carefully, then took out a small plastic bottle of Murine and rinsed out her eyes. Her face was puffy and red, and she ran the cold-water tap and splashed the water on her cheeks. Then she took a paper towel, soaked it, pressed it across her eyes. After a minute her stomach stopped jumping and she looked at herself. She took out mascara and did her eyes. She penciled on fresh eyebrows and put on a pale shade of lipstick.

She looked good. Her face was still tan from living in Santa Barbara and her blue eyes looked bright within the shadowed lashes. Her cheeks had color because of the crying. She laughed and took out her hairbrush. Stroking her hair calmed her like it always did.

She was sitting on a yellow couch by the big windows in the side lobby when Douglas came in. She was leafing through a magazine, and as he approached he noticed her hair was longer, fuller looking, and her face looked good, beautiful, happy.

Confused, he gave her a kiss, sat down hard on the couch, said he had only a few minutes to stay.

"Well," she said, "I guess I certainly have made a mess of things, haven't I?"

"We both have."

"It's not too late, is it? I mean, I really have changed. Back home I realized that I don't want to live my parents' life. I couldn't stand it there. I suppose you have contempt for me."

"No."

"I want to stay here. You were right. It is a lovely city. If things don't work out I'm prepared to stay and get a job. I mean, you can see me whenever you want, but I'll get a place of my own and stay out of your affairs."

"You can stay if you want," he said. "That's your right, but I don't think it would be fair to see you."

"Don't you love me?"

He sat for a moment.

"Yes," he said finally, "but I don't want to see you."

"That doesn't make sense.

"There's someone else."

"No," he said, "there isn't. It isn't that simple."

She persisted for a moment, then stopped suddenly, thinking of all the mistakes she had made, the time she had slashed his paintings, her frigidity.

He said he thought the best thing to do was put her on the train again and send her back home.

"I'm sorry, Gwen, I am. I don't want to be cruel, but I'm sorry. It just would be too difficult to have you here. Difficult for both of us."

They sat in silence and then she agreed, saying she had just enough money for train fare. He took out his wallet and gave her forty dollars.

"I don't need it," she said.

"Take it."

"I have enough money. I just wanted to see—"

"To see what?"

"Nothing," she said, feeling tears just beginning to start up behind her voice. "Would you have someone go upstairs and get my suitcase? Nothing is unpacked. Both my coat and suitcase are lying on the bed."

"Don't you want to stay one night, to rest up?"

"No. I'd like to leave now."

He stood up, asking what her room number was. She told him. He walked away toward the desk. She stood up, smoothed her skirt, then walked fast to the ladies' room. She felt dizzy and once inside she pushed open a toilet door and threw up into the bowl. She wiped her mouth with some paper then threw up again. The odor of her vomit assaulted her and other odors and she stood up, feeling better, yet drained, somehow outside her own body. She went to the outside door without washing her face. Douglas wasn't in the lobby. She went back in, cry-ing again. There was stuff on her blouse that she scraped at. It wouldn't come out. She drenched it in water and tried to stop crying. She tore her blouse, going wild for a moment.

"That filthy bastard," she said, "that filthy rotten bastard."

Gradually she calmed down, her mind going quiet, then clear. She stared at her face in the mirror.

"You're not a bad-looking girl," she said. "You're not at all."

She felt a charge of tension everywhere around her but not inside. She felt quiet inside. She brushed back her hair with her hand and then went out.

Douglas was standing by the couch, her coat draped over his arm. Her suitcase rested on the floor.

"I've called the airport," he said. "I've made reservations on a ten o'clock flight. Let's go out to dinner and maybe a movie."

"A movie," she said.

"Something," he said, "or walk around."

She took the coat from him, looking at his face, somehow looking at exactly what his face presented, capturing not his gestures or how he seemed to be, but exactly those few lines coming out from the corners of his eyes, lines she had never seen before, age lines, he had actually aged, she had never noticed it before.

"No," she said, "nothing. I don't think I'd like to wait. I'd like to catch the train."

"Are you sure?"

"Yes," she said.

"Are you all right?"

"Yes," she said. "You go on."

"I'm sorry," he said.

"So am I," she said.

"Does the train leave this afternoon? I mean is there one?"

"It doesn't matter," she answered. "Please go."

Country Wedding in the City

Then she walked over to the groom.

"You fuck you shit you piss ass stink! Blow my hole!"

"Weow!" said he. "Are you ever primed!"

"Good luck, George," friends called out.

Did they all live in the country?

Nope.

Only Dave, the best man. Dave owned a Peugeot. That afternoon he got in the back and shot up 500 mgs of paraboxelynic, flew out the window and slowly rose up over the city into the country fair air of the sky.

"Whatcha doing up there, Dave?" friends cried out.

Smilin', Dave waved.

Seize the Time

John, an active university revolutionary, learned Steven's ideas of the world were different from his. Since John liked Steven's style, his name, his ability to hustle chicks, he set out to educate Steven in revolutionary cause and rhetoric. Steven, he felt, would look good on the barricades.

Steven, however, resisted, insisting against John's personality. Yet he found himself naturally curious about a worldview of which he self-admittedly knew so little. And so, after a normal time resisting, Steven finally said, "Okay, I'll go to the next meeting of the collective. I've nothing to lose. If there I see that what you believe helps man to become a better man, I'll accept your arguments and join the movement."

John, however, when he heard this, far from being delighted, was deeply depressed, saying to himself, If Steven goes to a meeting, sees the inexperience on the faces of the kids, fails to see the humor in the almost inane repetition of all the raps going down, he'll end up thinking all revolutionary ideas are frauds.

Turning to Steven, he said, "No, man, it's not a good idea. Just listen to me, read what I have to give you, then think on it."

"No," Steven answered, "I want to see for myself."

A few nights later Steven sat in on a meeting. At first, listening to the dialogues, he formed no opinions. But after a time he began to see the aura of romance about the revolutionaries: the boldest speakers had the best-looking girls. And, as he listened, he formed the conclusion that, without exception, the better speakers were completely certain their viewpoints were right, were morally correct, that contrary to what they were asking for —justice—they condemned all men not on their side as traitors to mankind.

Steven was unhappy with what he saw. He left the meeting quietly, holding his complaints for an encounter with John.

They met the next day.

John, quickly scanning Steven's face, had not the slightest hope of his conversion. They had coffee together and talked of academic affairs, both avoiding any discussion of the movement. Finally, though, John could stand it no longer.

"So," he asked, "what happened at the meeting?"

"Well," Steven said, "what I saw was a bunch of guys romantically in love with themselves, and, far from being involved in dreams that would make them better human beings, I only saw the same old shit: cats looking to be admired by their peer group."

"I thought that would happen," John said.

"But," Steven continued, "what struck my imagination was that while the radicals were responding to new ideas in old human ways, it was obvious that the ideas they were trying to express were true and good; ideas that would hasten the end of a competitive society, notions of racial superiority, sound the death knell of the idea of heroes, leaders, supermen; ideas that would change the world for the good and joy of all, if enough people understood them.

"In short, by participating I was converted and freed."

"Wow," John said, smiling. He was suddenly the happiest of men. The revolution was working. Rushing Steven up from his seat, he took him across the street to the Id Bookstore and bought him a copy of Mao's thoughts.

When other revolutionaries heard of Steven's conversion they quickly became friends, solid friends. And right now, at almost any time of the day, you can go up on the Avenue to the U District and see Steven standing in the street, a red Mao button in his lapel, waiting for the revolution to come.

Stiff

Charley Winterbourne drinks muscatel up on the third floor. Like they say, he says, Goodnight, Chet, Goodnight, David, and Walter, Walter Cronkite when he says that's the way it was, Walter, Charley says. Charley sits stocking footed on the edge of the bed. He pours more wine into his glass. The wine pours gold and brown and clear. Walter, Walter Cronkite. Charley lifts his glass. No one else is in the room. Out the window the lights of San Francisco are yellow. The sky is a soft dark blue. Goodnight, folks, goodnight, that's the way it was. Charley still has his hat on. His grin is sleepy and he is sleepy too. Goodnight, Chet, Goodnight, David, and Walter, Walter Cronkite when he says, Goodnight, folks, goodnight.

Street

He was peddling speed and coke, a very flashy dealer in tapestry bell-bottoms, yellow ruffled shirt, leather coat, leather headband, long hair flowing down to his shoulders. We walked together for a minute going up past City Lights Bookstore.

"Naw, that's bullshit, man, 'cause I've been hassled with again. If they come they'd better come in pairs 'cause one isn't going to do it and if he shoots he'd better kill me 'cause I'll shoot the fucker if he misses and if he kills me then I'm free 'cause when you're dead you're free."

Then: "I want to be free and we can't be free as long as one of those pigs is alive."

Then: "No narc would come up here, man, 'cause if they did they'd be killed with fucking butcher knives."

Another cat with long hair and narrow stovepipe bells was standing at the corner waiting for the light. He overheard us.

"With machine guns, man," this guy said, "every fuckin' one of them."

Kid Colt Outlaw in Wyoming

The ghosts of a hundred Pawnee warriors glared eerily from the ancient Indian burial grounds. Kid Colt, senses alert, the sound of motion whipping his head, was advancing into a phantom ambush, the oil-black rain sky alive with the possibility of psychic death. Suddenly the Kid's mind flashed back to the strange events which led to this fateful encounter. Lightning bolted through the window onto the Kid's crib bars, dancing about, then shot into a light socket, leaving the Kid peacefully sleeping, the room empty of fury, while outside it rained, inside, the Kid's parents in shock had looked on, helpless to rescue the baby, it all took place so fast, and there was no need, strange child! A mystery to be unfolded! At eleven, strange currents said, Ask God to strike you dead, ask; at nineteen, Philosophy 101, some girl stood up saying, Who am I, so everyone laughed, everyone except the Kid then spreading his hands out into the inscrutable, while now, now, high above the clouds the unseen moon rose orangely over the earth, thus the evening found Kid Colt taking it all back home, hurtling through déjà vu, BAM! What was that? Ghosts, the Kid thought, looking back, don't make noise. Something there was melting into the shadows. Wind was howling over the mesa. Then it happened! The Yamaha seized up! The back tire skidding out, screaming, he slid! Quick as a flash the Kid kicked it out of gear, controlled the slide, popping the clutch, headlight flaring dimly in the rain. He stopped and stomped. It wouldn't kick over. He tried again. Voices floated to him: Kid, Kid, the spirits of the Pawnee were with you tonight, white brother, we saw you fight with the weapons of warriors long dead, all are grateful. The Kid dismounted, pushing up his visor, his breath fogging the air. He started rolling the bike off into the brush, the search for America breaking down, his real journey about to commence. Desperately, he longed for a Standard Station.

Sather Gate

She was a non-student, a runaway from smalltown lowclass Oklahoma, she said, come to Berkeley she didn't know why, her boyfriend was into an off-the-wall movie trip, like we were into this thing where the camera is your brother so you're free to do anything, do any thing, every thing you can think of, a sex thing, everybody was up on acid, and I began thinking, Shit, man, we're into this thing where all learning is considered good, like that brought us the hydrogen bomb, you know.

Later, leaving her apartment, That's the real problem, she said, it's too damn bad everything has to be so casual.

Early Morning Wind

I n a terrible snowstorm when John was a boy they had brought a donkey-steam engine up that road and down into the creek bed, the hollar. John told that at the supper table, eating pan-fried chicken, beans, green salad. John's farm was clean. Sarah had never seen the ocean. She asked Lee to send her some shells from the ocean, seashells. John said, "Well, we'll go see the old place in the morning."

They rode on John's big-wheeled tractor out along a high bank on a tilt along a long, high-staked turkeyfence, the turkeys all running hard and banging into each other when John crashed the horn. "They agitate me so I agitate them," he said.

It was a bright morning with the sky blue and the grass dry and dusty. The road disappeared as they came to what looked like a small farmhouse. Woods started in the back of the house and went away as far as you could see in a covering of endless hills. John stopped the tractor and got off. A man came out of the house to the fence.

"Morning," John said. "This here's my cousin's grandson from out west. I'd like to take him back into the hollar and show him where the old place was."

"Sure enough, John," the man said. He unlocked the padlock on the aluminum gate and let them through.

The road broke immediately into some trees, the tractor jouncing and shaking. Lee tried to imagine running a horse through. His grandfather had worn a diamond ring on his little finger and had a racing horse, the only one to go to school, too, the baby of the family. As they went on, Lee got John to talk about him. "They didn't call him that," John said, "they called him Faye, he was sure enough a rounder, one thing I recall was when he'd got himself and his guitar up in one of them limestone caves up near the ridge and started hooing in there at the boys out working in the corn around the bend—when they heard that sound they just took off, wasn't till the afternoon that your great granddad rounded them up and when he found out it was Faye that had done it he gave him a solid whippin'—a rounder, for sure, that was him . . ."

The rest of the trip continued rough, yet beautiful, they followed a barely discernable road, more a track, along the hillsides, often driving around huge boulders and fallen trees, and then they turned down and were in a draw where they went along a dry creek bed that wound around between wooded cliffs. John told him it might be hard to believe, but that back in the eighteen-nineties and during the turn of the century a lot of folks lived on those hillsides, farming down here in the bottom, hundreds of folks. It was hard to believe. The slopes were straight up and down in places, entirely covered with growth of all kinds. There were no houses nor did it look as if there ever could have been.

After a time the creek bed opened into a near valley, about a hundred yards wide. John stopped the tractor and shut it off. The sound of thousands of cicadas droned off the hills. They walked across the dry rounded stones of the creek bed and went over to the slope. Lee had lost all sense of direction. It was extremely hot. John pointed left, high along the hillside.

"The big house was up there," he said. "That was the second house, the one I remember as a boy."

"Where was the first?"

"Right where you're standing," John said.

He showed Lee the outlines of the foundation. Actual square-cut blocks of limestone brought from Rogers forty miles away. The blocks were still in the ground, dirted over. Lee cleaned one off with the toe of his boot.

"Three kids in this house, the other eight up there," John said.

That was all there was to it. They walked up to where the cornfield had been and then came back to the tractor.

The next day John and Sarah took Lee into Claymore and then down to Rogers to see a man named Harnish. He'd been a pal of Faye's and was now in the VA Hospital. John said maybe he could tell him more about the old days.

The VA Hospital was new looking, recently constructed. The lawns looked old, though, and rich. They went inside and down a broad corridor. Harnish was in the end ward. The room was pleasant and sunny. Harnish was sitting up in his bed, two white pillows behind his back. Lee expected an old-looking man and was surprised. Harnish's face was lean and tan and his hair was dark with only flecks of gray in it.

"Bill," John said.

"Hello, John."

"Bill, this here is Lee Hatcher, Faye Hatcher's boy's boy. You remember Faye?"

"Sure," Harnish said. "I do." He was silent for a moment, then he said, "It's bad, John, they've got to operate."

"Well," John said, "they'll do all right."

"No, John, they won't."

"Sure they will."

"No, it's terminal, John."

"I don't believe that, Bill," Sarah said.

"Don't tell Judy now. She doesn't know."

"Has she been here?"

"No, I haven't let her."

On the way back John pulled into a Dairy Queen drive-in and bought them all double-decker ice cream cones. Sarah told Lee a nice story about Bill and Faye that she had heard of and then one about her grown kids and how Laurie, who would be Lee's cousin twice removed, had learned about how babies were made and had him and herself laughing.

That evening after supper John asked Lee to come outside with him and he'd show him the main barn, the only thing he hadn't gotten around to doing. John was a large man, nearly six three and easily two hundred and thirty pounds. He'd worn Big Mac overalls, a blue work shirt, and a felt hat all four days Lee stayed there, even on the visit to the hospital. He was dressed this way now and Lee studied him as they walked out across the lawn and then into the barnyard. John was dark like Grandfather Hatcher had been, all the Hatchers had Indian blood in them.

They went inside the barn and John walked over to a stall, then turned around.

"Well, Lee, it's been real nice havin' you stay with us."

"Thank you, John. I've learned a lot."

"Tell me one thing, Lee. It's something I've been meaning to ask you. You don't have the true faith do you?"

"No, sir," Lee said. "You mean the Baptist, don't you?"

"Yes, sir, I do."

"No, not right now," Lee answered.

"Have you any faith?"

"No, sir, I guess I don't."

"You think about it, son. It would make this old man mighty happy to think that someday you would."

"All right, John," Lee said, "I will think about it."

"It would make me mighty happy," John said.

"I'll try my best, John."

Becky: West Florida Romance

"That's them," Reeves said.

Down the highway under some trees some people stood by a white mailbox. The little girl was standing behind the woman. A boy in a T-shirt stood next to the girl. They both looked small, babies, really.

I looked at Reeves. His alcoholic's face was up over the wheel with his eyes squinted, trying to see through the dirty windshield and glare off the highway. Fine veins branched redly under his cheeks. He was excited for sure.

We went off the road and along the shoulder.

"Becca'll ride up here with us," he said. "You'll see what I mean."

We came alongside and he stopped the car.

"Well," he said out my window, "I made it after all."

"I knew you would," the woman said. "I wasn't worried."

"That's good," Reeves said.

The woman smiled at me and pulled the children forward. Her hair was bleached, the roots showing dark. Her eyebrows were painted on, like those I had seen in photographs of Mexican whores in boxes outside Mexico City around the turn of the century.

"C'mon, Paul," she said, tugging at the boy. He resisted, apparently scared of me. His face was dirty and he wore thick spectacles, his eyes large and milky-blue behind the glass. The woman pushed him forward, then the little girl.

"This here's a Washington boy," Reeves said. "Picked him up outside Lassiter."

"Pleased to meet you," the woman said. She pushed the boy again, and I reached over and opened the back door.

Reeves leaned over the seat and as the little girl got in he lifted her up over and stood her between us.

The woman then the boy got in and I closed their door.

"This sure is good of you, Pat," the woman said.

"How's my ol' Becca?" Reeves said. He laid his arm around the child's waist. "Can you give your ol' Uncle Pat a kiss? Hmmm? Can you?"

The girl was looking at me, her head slightly above mine, her eyes clear child's eyes. She was a beautiful little girl.

Reeves put his hand on her leg.

I shook my head at her.

"The bank closes at three, don't it?" the woman asked.

Reeves pulled Becca to him. She put her arm around his neck.

"Ain't she somethin'," he said.

Becca gave him a kiss. Reeves moved his hand up under her dress. She kissed again and started to bounce up and down on the seat, the cushion gently moving beneath me.

"Well, Pat," I said, "I believe you. I think I'll get out here if you don't mind. I'd like to walk a bit."

"Out here?" Reeves said, looking over Becca's shoulder. He had a perplexed look on his face.

"Right," I said. I opened the door and got out. In back the woman was looking in her purse. She looked up, startled.

"Sure," Reeves said. He reached around Becca and closed the door.

I stepped back.

Becca didn't look, watching Reeves as he took the wheel. Then the car moved off, bouncing as it hit the pavement, sun flashing sharply off its dusty flanks. The boy's face appeared at the rear window, soon vanishing into shadow.

I watched them for a moment and then turned around and walked over to the mailbox.

Leona Pride, it read. "A widow woman," Reeves had said. "Yes, sir, really honest to God in love, the both of us. No, she don't know. She thinks it's her I'm interested in."

War Songs

I've been thinking of you and hope you have a Happy Birthday tomorrow. Hope the day is correct. I told Gloria how we used to have mental telepathy in Spokane, ha, ha.

Hope Jay is well and I have wondered if you got over the ulcer trouble. Hope Dave is well and happy. Do they have children? Excuse the mistakes. My glasses need changing as I don't see too good. I remember Martha's daughter Lynn and what caused her to die so young? That must have been very hard on Martha and family.

Mother and Melissa have been fine. Fred is about the same (bedridden), he is up a little each day. I told you about his broken neck and he never walked again. Donna gets pretty tired from the care. She had to train about like a nurse to care for him. Rena Jean lives in Tacoma. She has two girls. Diane lives at Skyway has two boys and one girl. Betty and Lora had some nerve trouble. Betty is fine but Lora isn't too well yet. Think Tom is a lot to blame. David (their boy) just twenty-one eloped with a Japanese girl and the dad and other grandma disowned him. Lora and Tom bought a new model home at Bothell and Tom won't let him bring her there at all. The rest of us will be kind to her if that's what he wants. Lora is a Christian and will be good to her. I don't approve of mixed marriages but will always be good to her. He met her at the University of Wash.

I was very sad about the middle of November. John's brother Ralph had a heart attack. He lived just a few days and passed away. We got two cute cards to send him at the Veterans' Hospital in Walla Walla and had some pictures for him too but he died before I got them there. He was still Catholic so they had a rosary and mass. I couldn't go as I was low on money. He was like a brother to me all these years. He was up to Davenport in August and helped Walter do some painting. He got diabetes and I know that he had been doctoring. Walter and Helen and families went to Walla Walla for the funeral. On the way home they got about twenty miles from Walla Walla and Walter had a heart attack at the wheel. Mike took over (he is eighteen now) and they took Walter to the hospital. He didn't have any heart damage. The electric card-o-graph showed the old arteries ruptured and the new ones took over. I told you he had heart surgery a year ago, I believe. Had he not had the operation he would have died on the spot. We had two heart attacks within two weeks in the family and you can imagine how upset I was—after going through it with John. The Walla Walla heart doctors who did the surgery seem to think he is getting along okay Doris (John's sister) isn't very well her blood pressure went high and she had chest pains from the strain of it all. Wish I could go visit them. I haven't been to Walla Walla for six years or Davenport.

Guess you think this is some letter with all the bad news. I am just getting over a virus. It started in my stomach and then I got a sore throat I lost my voice and it hit my lungs and I nearly had pneumonia for a week or two. I have been several weeks getting over the bronchial cough and cold. I had been planning to write for several weeks. I felt pretty bum.

Donald took Gloria on a long trip in August she was gone all month. She was in Wash., Idaho, Montana, Yellowstone, S. Dakota, Nebraska, Missouri, Arkansas, Tennessee (saw Elvis Presley's home in Memphis), New Orleans, Texas, Dallas, New Mexico (saw the Carlsbad Caverns), Nevada, Las Vegas, Reno, Northern Calif., Ore., and home. They stayed at motels with pools and TV and she had the time of her life. We sure missed her though. She and Julie both had mumps this summer.

Do you ever hear from any of the Bureau of Reclamation people or from the Corps of Engineers? Think of some often.

Heard "If I Loved You" and "Stranger in Paradise" yesterday, war songs. Thought of Mitch. I have never got over that.

Wish you could come over sometime would love to see you. Don't think I thanked you for the lovely fruitcake. It sure was nice to have and I use the tin for a cookie jar.

Love,

Klamath Falls

Mark stood up and held out his hand. The car was a pickup, dull red with a camper on the back. An old man was driving, no one else with him. Bill sat down and watched. Mark was waving his arm up and down. The pickup went past, then slowed, the red brake lights flashing on, off.

"Let's go, man," Mark said, grabbing his pack. He started running.

Bill got up, taking his pack through one of the loops. He ran halfway, then slowed to a walk. Nosed over on the shoulder, the pickup was running, its tail end sticking out on the highway. Mark was at the cab opening the door.

"Morning," Bill heard Mark say. "How far you going?"

"Morning," came the answer.

Bill walked up behind Mark. The driver looked at him.

"Where you boys going?"

"K. Falls," Mark said.

"The both of you?"

"Right," Mark said.

"Well, that's just fine. Hop on in."

"You going up there?" Bill said.

"Up near there."

"Great," Mark said. He stepped on the running board and swung in, sliding across the seat.

"C'mon, man," he said to Bill.

Bill climbed up and got in, keeping his pack on his lap. He closed the door. The inside of the cab had a sour smell, a mixture of gasoline and rust and old food.

"All set?" asked the driver.

"Yep," Mark answered.

"Good. Here we go."

He let out the clutch and the pickup lurched ahead, starting for the ditch then cutting sharply for the highway.

"Man," Bill said.

"Been waiting long?" asked the driver.

"All night," said Mark. "We're going back to school. We've been out on spring vacation."

"Is that so?" the driver said. "My name's Billy. Billy Wetzel."

"Mark," Mark said, "and that's Bill."

"Pleased to meet you. It's a privilege to meet such nice-looking boys."

Bill looked at him. Underneath that blue baseball cap he was fruity looking, all right, weak, his mouth crumpled in without any teeth.

"Thank you," Mark said.

Bill said nothing. He took off his coat, wadded it up, put it against the window. He slumped over against it and closed his eyes, listening to the sound of the engine pulling them steadily on.

"You boys ever do any posing?" It was the old man's voice.

"Posing?" Mark asked. "You mean modeling?"

"No," said the old man, "posing."

"Artists?"

"No, people."

"How's that?"

"Tables, you see, you walk—"

"Tables." Mark laughed. "You mean walk around with no clothes on—"

"That's it."

". . . in front of a bunch of people?"

"That's it."

"Ha," Mark laughed. "How about you, Bill?"

"Shit," Bill said. He closed his eyes again. He knew it. He knew it all along. He could tell by the way the pickup had approached.

Mark laughed again.

"It ain't so hard," the old man said. "Pays good money too."

"Tell me about it," Mark said. "I mean, what do you do?"

"You walk around these tables—"

"Who's there? I mean, is it just men or women or what?"

"Everybody. All kinds of people."

"Shoot." Mark laughed. "Don't you feel kind of funny?"

"Oh no," the old man said. "Why should you? They pay you. It's just work."

"Yeah, but I mean, well, what do they do? Just look at you?"

"Some of them."

"Jesus," Bill said, "that's sick."

"Why, hell," the old man said, "I've even had guys pay me ten dollars jus' so's they could kiss my belly. You ever had your belly kissed?"

He was looking at Bill.

"Fuck, no," Bill said, "and I'd kill any son of a bitch that tried."

Mark laughed.

The old man looked away. Bill stared at him, then sat back. He expected Mark to say something. Mark would. Mark would say or do anything.

"You know, son," the old man said, "you're a lucky boy."

"Why?" Mark asked.

"No, not you. The other fellow."

"How's that?" Bill sat up. The old man was looking out at the road, both hands on the wheel.

"You've got a lovely set of teeth, sir——"

"Ha," Mark laughed.

"A blessing, you bet your life it is."

Bill looked at him, then sat back again, closing his eyes.

"Why is that?" Mark said.

"No taste," said the old man. "You can't taste a damn thing."

"Is that right?" Mark said.

"That's true," the old man said. "Makes you like a little baby again."

"I see," Mark said.

"Can't eat anything solid."

Mark didn't answer that and the voices stopped. There wasn't any talking for some time. Bill felt himself almost go to sleep. He opened his eyes. They were going up a long, slow grade with huge pines lining the sides. Up ahead, pools of light formed mirages on the blacktop.

"Yes, sir," the old man said, "pretty country up here."

"It is," Mark agreed.

"I always enjoy it. I come up here all the time."

"Where you from?"

"Mission Beach, down in San Diego."

"That's a long ways," Mark said.

"I'm always on the road, one time or another."

"You pick up many hitchhikers?"

"Always do," the old man said. "Last summer I picked up a fellow from Harvard. Spent six weeks together."

"No kidding," Mark said.

"Nice fellow. Just graduated. Went all the way to Canada with me. You ever been up there? Most of it's still virgin country, you know."

"That's what I understand," Mark said.

"You boys drink beer?"

They crested the grade and started around a curve. The right front wheel went off the pavement.

"Jesus," Bill said.

The old man let off the gas and slowed the truck. The curves fed into one another and then they were going down a long, sloping straight and then onto a long, white concrete bridge. Far below was a creek, brown-green between its banks.

"Sure," Mark said. "That's really pretty down there."

"It is," the old man answered. "Not good for much, though. Too many people use it."

"Yeah, I suppose so," Mark said.

"You've got to pack back into the mountains to get real country."

"I guess that's so," said Mark. "I'd like to do that. So would Bill."

"By myself," Bill said.

"What?"

"By myself," Bill repeated.

"Hey," Mark said, "I thought you were asleep. Sorry, man."

"No," Bill said.

"You boys got sleeping bags? You'd need sleeping bags to do that."

"No, not this trip," Mark said. "We've been visiting friends down in Berkeley. We didn't expect to have to sleep out."

"Couldn't go back in the mountains without good bags."

They went along another curve, the road well shadowed by the trees, only a narrow swath of blue sky over them.

"You boys ever been to San Francisco?"

"Sure," Mark said. "How about it, Bill?"

"Ever go into bars there?"

"We're not old enough to drink," Bill said.

"There's one place there you should see," the old man said, "just one big room."

"What for?" Mark asked.

"Couples," the old man said, "ten couples every night. All's they have in there is one light and a rug, a nice thick rug, nothing else . . ."

"Nothing else?"

". . . just one tiny light on, way down at the end, and a few cushions. No chairs, no tables, nothing . . ."

"Wow," Mark said, "what happens?"

"You name it."

"You mean balling?"

"Everything," the old man said, "sucking, fucking, switching . . ."

"I see," Mark said.

"Doors open at ten and stay open till there's ten couples then they close till six in the morning. No one can get in or get out until six."

"What's it cost?"

"Ten bucks a person."

"Two hundred bucks a night," Mark said.

"Every night," said the old man.

"That's a lot of dough."

"It's a lot of fun."

"I bet," Mark said. "I bet it is."

"You boys have to stop?"

Bill looked away from him. Coming toward them on the right was a clearing in the trees and a service station.

"Not me," Bill said.

"Sure," Mark said. "I could stand to wash up."

"I've got to," said the old man. He pumped the brakes and turned the wheel. They went off the highway into the station lot. He stopped at the side of the building.

"Coming?" He shut off the engine.

"Right," Mark answered.

The old man opened his door and got out. As he walked around the front of the truck he looked in at them. He was a lot bigger than Bill had thought he was. From a distance he didn't look so old. Bill watched him go over to the men's room at the back of the building.

"Well?" Mark said.

"Fuck you," Bill said. He opened his door.

"What the hell's wrong?"

"You figure it out," Bill said.

"Okay, man, that's all right with me."

"Okay." Bill lifted his pack and stepped down.

"I kind of feel sorry for the old coot, you know."

"Well, you know what to do." Bill put on his pack.

"What does that mean?"

"Go on in there."

"Where?"

"In the head, man, in the head."

"Look, Bill . . ."

"Look, nothing, Mark. All you have to do is split for the head. That'll cinch it for you. He'll take you to the moon."

"You're really an asshole, Bill, you know that?"

"Me!" Bill said. "Ha!"

"I said I was sorry, man. I am. It was a mistake."

Bill looked at him.

"You know, man," said Mark, "you don't know shit. You don't know the first goddamned thing about people."

"I'm learning pretty fast," Bill said, "I know that."
"You've got a lot more to learn, man."
"We'll see," Bill said. "We'll fucking see."
"Okay, take off."
"I am, man."
"All right," Mark said.

Bill walked back along the side of the pickup and then out toward the road. There weren't any cars coming. The highway was empty. He hoped one would come soon. He didn't want to be standing when Billy and Mark went by. What a rotten trip this had been. It really had.

"But not me," Bill said fiercely. "Not me."

The Big Apple

Their first time in Manhattan they stayed with Felicia's college roommate, Dolores, and her roommate, a good-looking boy named Gary.

The second night there, Gary, who had been gone all evening, came back to the flat with a man named Morton. Morton was about thirty-five years old and wore a gray suit. Dolores was away visiting an aunt and uncle somewhere up on Long Island and Gary and Morton slept together in Dolores's bed. David lay awake listening to them.

"It makes me sick," he said.

"Ssh," Felicia said. "Live and let live, babe."

"Not me," David said, "I'm getting the fuck out of here. I hate this goddamn place."

Felicia reached out and held on.

"Come back here, you silly," she said.

She kissed his arm and pulled him back down. "Listen," she said, "you know that I know Gary from school, don't you? Do you know that?"

"No," David said.

"Well, I do," Felicia said. "And I worry about him. I used to worry about him a lot. He's had some pretty horrible things happen to him. His mother slept with him until he was sixteen. Did I tell you I slept with him once? I think I'm the only girl he's ever slept with."

"No," David said, "you didn't tell me. Did it make any difference? He seems pretty happy the way he is."

"Not like us," she said. "Now here, come here, let's be happy too."

Army

Carol Ann came in, mildly ripped, happy in her eyes. Where is that boy, she said, ough, god damn him, I'm going to eat that boy up when he gets here, love, yes I love him, I love everybody, people are everything, aren't they, what else is there, sex, what else have I got going for me except my body, drugs, she laughed, her eyes full of secrets, old age, no, I'm not afraid of old age, everybody gets old, what do you expect, no, the only thing I'm afraid of is obsolescence, I'm afraid of getting obsolete, no one has to do that, no one, now repeat after me, women know more than men, repeat, women know more than men. We laughed together, she went out the door into the street.

Lucy in the Sky

S tanding up, head tipped forward, listening (Gray, a twenty-
three-year-old college graduate surfing until he is drafted, not
to the Vietnamese war, yet he would like to see a war. Blond, mod-
erately long hair, tan, Levi's, sky-blue deck shoes, striped red and
white shirt), mind jammed with the sensory impressions of this
house: its colored crystal prisms strung by wire across the windows,
its psychedelic-rock music posters on the walls, the mauve and rose
and cream scarves partitioning the room that gently billow from
second to second as wind comes in the open window behind Hansen sitting in a lotus on the couch—all of this a newness alien from
the old of surfboards and Goodwill mattresses on the bare floors
and surf pictures on the walls of the old surf house where he lived
while going to school when Hansen, two years ago, age eighteen,
first came on the scene having left his parents' home and moved
in (that surf house gone now in an urban renewal project that in
a year would not only have demolished the row of similar houses
on Ventura Point but will, because of a long, high, stone and steel
and concrete seawall, outrider of a planned six-story concrete and
palm-surrounded resort hotel, destroy the rock and sand forma-
tions of an ancient river mouth made point break, a peeling sym-
metrical surf break that provides on a strong west swell power rides
up to an eighth of a mile long, waves that give a rider an ecstatic
pride in his own courage in riding them; rides that Gray feels are
the major accomplishments of an already long athletic career; rides
that so far are the best moments of his life), seeking, Gray felt,
his friendship, his approval—all of this a newness overlaid by one
other impression: the hypodermic syringe lying on the white of
Hansen's kitchen sink; hearing now Hansen speak in answer to his
warning about being hustled by queers while hitchhiking north,
hearing Hansen now say, "So, it's all the same, man; it'd be a new
trip," blinked, paused, got a mindflash of darkness and the highway

and some forty-five-year-old fag unzipping Hansen's fly, and then, suddenly, totally, finally (at once thinking of Hansen's favorite saying, "Whatever happens, man, happens. It's all up to the stars.") understood him, understood why he always fell off in hard sections of hard waves, understood why he wasn't surfing anymore, understood why he had gone AWOL, understood the dope dealing, the turning on of his thirteen-year-old brother, understood the syringe, understood exactly where Hansen was; felt excited by the insight, relieved of any further curiosity, and disgusted enough to say, "Well, man, we're going up to Stanley's if you want a ride to get you started and right now I'm going outside 'cause if the police really are coming it could be anytime and I sure as hell don't want to be here when they do."

"Wow, man!" said Hansen.

Hoefer, looking at Gray, said nothing.

Gray, wanting somehow to undo the harshness of his own statement, looked up out the window, looked back at Hansen, then picked up the binoculars off the couch and brought them up to his eyes, looking beyond the two blocks of tract housing, a field, the gray-ribboned freeway, focusing them for distance on California Street, seeing moving into clarity off the dark brown of the upper parking lot beyond the two squat silver Shell Oil storage tanks the long gray-green walls, six, seven, eight, more stacked out toward the horizon, the first good wave breaking maybe two hundred yards out across the high tide, its face a solid six foot, maybe seven, but too much wind, way too much, sections pushing over everywhere along its line. Gray jumped to the fourth wave, still smooth looking, a good five-footer starting to peak over, made the opening turn, stayed high in the pocket by the white now breaking, then drove down the green and out, setting up to make a hard turn back up. The long bulging wall ahead collapsed, turning over into whitewater.

"Stanley's the only place," Gray said, looking back at Hansen, seeing Hansen smiling, thinking then, He's freaked out, seeing Hansen's Indian moccasins, his rotten Levi's laden with iron-on patches, the faded cloth a soft white blue, the patches green, jean blue, dark blue, wheat, black, solid over both knees and up the thighs, pants Gray thought of as part of Hansen's new doper style (but not that, not style in the usual mode of unusual dress for gaining attention but a style pronounced by a girl at a recent party, saying, "Those are your soul pants, right?" "Yeah, right," Hansen had said, liking her, liking that she had defined it for him, seeming to know that he had *created* the pants: had washed and sewed and ironed them; had ironed then sewed on each patch actually working on them everywhere in town; had slowly welded and pressed them into his psyche under a variety of mostly steam irons everywhere, Grandma's, Mom's, a girl's, even Gray's new place; with each new tear had ironed on patch after patch after patch until, simply, they weren't cloth pants any longer but were flesh, his flesh), pants that didn't fit with the athletic look of the hard, tan belly and chest and shoulders, pants that were one more bad omen for Hansen's future, pants that matched the ruined, blood-reddened whites of Hansen's eyes now looking into his; Gray thinking then, What a handsome guy, what a dumb fuck, why feel sorry for that; then looked at Hoefer sitting impassively in the armchair, running his hand through his beard, obviously not seeing that Hansen was simply fucked, Why, Gray thought, even bother talking with the guy? If he doesn't care, he doesn't care.

"I'll be down in a minute," Hoefer said, seeing that Gray was asking him to leave.

"Okay," Gray said. He tossed the binoculars next to Hansen, glanced at a Day-Glo orange-and-pink-bordered black poster of a tall, skull grinning, white skeleton draped in a garland of roses announcing THE GRATEFUL DEAD, AVALON, SAN FRANCISCO, thought symbolically, That figures, and said:

"See you, Hans."

"Okay," Hansen answered.

As Gray turned and walked out the door, twisting to avoid the last scarf, looking ahead to the dark well of carpeted stairway going down to the street, sensing the age and decay of the house, remembering then not clearly the visual picture (the slowness of it, the absolute concentration, the pulling of the red into thin, clean glass then the gentle, steady, perfect push back) but thinking mostly of the shock he had felt when watching one of Hansen's new buddies shoot tranks at a party a week ago, remembering how the kid (another guy who wasn't surfing much anymore) had smiled afterward, softly, quietly, some kind of weirdly beautiful light in his eyes, not looking up at Gray, it seemed, although his eyes had been fixed on him, but seeming to be looking up at something else, someone else directly behind Gray, although there had been no one there, Hoefer sighed, and Gray, hearing him, thought, What the hell is Hoefer going to do? There's nothing he can do.

In a minute Gray was gone and Hansen, still grinning, shrugged and shook his head.

"Well," Hoefer said, "queers are a pretty strange trip, you know."

"Ah, I was just jiving," said Hansen. "What's his problem anyway?"

"I don't know."

"He really gets uptight sometimes," Hansen said.

"Well," said Hoefer, "not that it's any of my business but what's the deal on that needle? You use that thing?"

Hansen threw out his hands.

"Bad karma, man."

"Yeah, you're right."

"Sure," Hoefer said.

Hansen grinned.

"Listen, you ass, why don't you wait a couple of days? C'mon out to my place. We'll ride Rincon tomorrow when the tide's better."

"No, I better not."

"I can dig it," Hoefer said, deciding to leave. He stood up. "Seeing some country'll be good for you."

"Yeah," Hansen said, "and save my ass, too."

"It will."

"I know."

"Okay," Hoefer said.

"You want to share a number before you split?"

"Well," Hoefer laughed. "Sure." He sat down. "Gray brought me up here to get you off the dope, you know."

"Well," Hansen said, "the dope."

"The dope," Hoefer laughed, "sure."

Hansen got up, going past into the kitchen. Hoefer heard the oven door open, close.

"Your stash in there?"

"Part of it," Hansen said. He came back in carrying a cellophane bag of dark, wet-looking grass. "The rest is up in Santa Barbara. You want this stuff? It doesn't taste too good."

"No, not now."

"Yeah, take it, man. I'll put it out back. You can swing by later and pick it up."

"How much you want for it?"

"Nothing, man. It's a gift. I can't use it. I'm splitting for sure. It's jail time around here, you know. I can't dig that. My name is on the list. I've got to go."

"Well," Hoefer said, "yeah, wow, okay Where'll you put it?"

Hansen was looking down into the bowl of a dark, curved pipe. He didn't answer for a moment.

"Out by the fence. You know that chain-link fence by the freight office? I'll bury it there at the corner."

"Good," Hoefer said, watching Hansen push a finger down into the bowl.

"Here," Hoefer said, getting up. He struck a match and held it over the bowl.

Hansen inhaled, sucking the flame down.

"I'd heard that things were hot," Hoefer said, "no pun intended." He sat down next to Hansen. "I thought I'd come by and see what was going on." Then he laughed. "No, man, really to get your new stick. Are you taking it? I mean, you're not hitchhiking with it, are you?"

"Yeah," Hansen said, passing the pipe, speaking without letting out smoke, talking up against the top of his throat, "my little brother has it, but go ahead. Tell him I said you could use it. You'll really dig on it. Yater really knows what he's doing."

"Good," Hoefer said. "It'll work good in this swell." He looked at the pipe in his hand. "Listen, man, what's with your needle trip, like I don't understand that."

"That's nothing," Hansen said, "it's just a thing like all the guys in the brig were on to it and this one guy from L.A. liked me so he gave me the spike, a totally spaced-out dude, you know, it's no big thing."

"Okay," Hoefer said, taking a toke.

"It's cool," Hansen said. He took the pipe.

"I mean, like it's a little scary, you know."

"Listen, Hoef," Hansen said, "I'm into a good thing."

"Yeah?" said Hoefer, watching the side of Hansen's face, looking at his eyes.

"God," Hansen said, still not letting the air out of his lungs. He considered that expression. "Yeah," he said.

"God?"

"God . . ." Hansen was saying again, giving Hoefer the pipe. Hoefer took another toke, closing his eyes at the burn hitting the back of his throat, smelling the sweet, harsh reek. ". . . like I think I got really close."

"Yeah?" Hoefer opened his eyes, letting out the smoke, seeing no color, feeling the warmth, his thought taken by God, the word, enjoying the word, feeling from it a moment of sensation like a church thought, the smoke rolling in his brain, the invisible host, laughing at that pun, feeling that laugh as a moment of quiet and calm that made things (now looking past Hansen onto the rose color of a scarf dappled with shadow and weight and space, feeling too, the space between Hansen and the rose, both floating) seem musical, full of wonder, near to that feeling, the pure feeling that often sitting in his church gave him . . .

"I'm not thinking God thoughts at all now, man," Hansen said, "and it's a real bringdown, you know what I mean? I mean, there's this giant hassle at me now so I've got to cool it for a while, right?"

"Yeah," Hoefer agreed, "that's right," thinking, Yes, it is, it is a God feeling, it must be (at eighteen at his father's insistence, he had driven off the coast to Utah and Brigham Young University, driven there in a '56 Caddy-powered '34 Ford Tudor with his Velzy-Jacobs racked on the top, starting higher education full of fear and rebellion, feeling ill-prepared and stifled, wanting no more formal education now that high school was over, not even wanting to see what the university had to offer, hating first the climate and then the rigidity of studying, feeling there was little hope of success for him in either the temporal or the spiritual world there, longing for the coast, the sea, missing his true satisfaction: the pump and lift of surf excitement shooting adrenaline into him seventy, eighty times a day, and so left the first time he received what he wanted, a failing grade on his first English composition exam, this three weeks after he enrolled, and came back to the coast to be tossed out of the home, then—he sold the car—going on his own, surfing through that winter, ending at the sea's edge, living under the Malibu Pier during the summer of '59, beginning a career based on hundreds and thousands of hours spent in the water: creator of the best rides ever seen at Secos and some at Malibu and Rincon, too: solitary, unique, magical performances, his whole land appearance based on his role as a performer, full hair and beard, shaggy cutoff sleeveless woman's fur coat, flamboyant shirts and pants, never shoes, always dark glasses: rides that made him a star in high school auditorium sixteen-millimeter surf movies, earned him board endorsements and free trips to Hawaii and always work in nearly any surfboard shop on the California coast; rides that gave him for more than nine years a strong sense of self-worth, this sense arrogantly based, a complete hang-everything-else sense, a sense necessary to develop his skill; and rides done on hundreds of days spent totally stoned, first smoking marijuana that first summer at Malibu, marijuana becoming both a sacrament of his free existence and part of his pre-performance ritual, then a part of the joy of riding, a way of taking himself into his own body, but then quit two years ago at the age of twenty-seven after being rejected in love, had turned back to the church and his family, started work full time, won the girl back, married her, then started again, even though he felt he shouldn't, because, as he told her, telling her this while he was stoned, she wasn't, "a tool for seeing the divine, like out there now"—both of them standing together on the beach at Oil Piers looking out along the pier seeing a wave silently loom up under the strutwork, dark, then emerald green, taking in sunlight through the back, diffusing it, spreading it in a moving glow gliding steadily toward them, all translucent along its face, all green motion and form—"I can feel the whole weight of that wave actually moving through my head, I mean feel it, its reality, and can merge into it becoming one with that moving part of the entire breathing apparatus of the planet . . .") the same feeling. "You know, man," Hoefer said, "I get it in church. You ought to go to church with me. Why don't you?"

"I mean," Hansen said, "it was with my little brother, you know, like I'd dropped a tab and went out at C Street and Donny was out and we started paddling up to Stables without saying anything, it was just like that, we looked at one another and I went into it, like, well . . . wow . . ."

"Yeah," Hofer said, giving the pipe back.

"You want some? I'll lay some on you."

"Acid?"

"Yeah."

"No, man," said Hoefer, "I already know, you see."

He shook his head at the offered pipe.

"You sure?"

"I know." Hoefer laughed. "That's what I said."

Hansen laughed. He took another toke off the pipe, then dumped the ashes out the window. "Bye," he said.

"Right." Hoefer laughed. "That's it, you know. It's a groovy feeling."

"It was really beautiful," Hansen said, "like all I had to do was remember, you know, just remember."

"So?"

"So?"

"So you didn't remember." Hoefer laughed.

"Right." Hansen laughed, both now laughing together, Hansen at one time Hoefer's follower, a would-be surf mag, surf flick star, had wanted to accomplish in two years what Hoefer had taken six years to accomplish, had style, good wave judgment but no ability to finish, had fallen off on critical waves in three critical Single A contests and so decided he had no gift, Hansen now in this easy laughter feeling himself to be, for the first time, finally, Hoefer's equal, and Hoefer feeling it too, both suddenly happy in their new understanding of each other.

"But I'll get it again," Hansen said, "I will."

Outside, Gray sat in Hoefer's panel truck, feet up on the dash, idly watching the after-work traffic. The freeway entrance three blocks ahead was jammed and two rows of cars were slowly rolling past the panel, feeding into the entrance. Gray was thinking about Stanley's, wondering what kind of shape its wave would have, wondering whether the swell was too big for it, and thinking about Stanley's took him into thinking about Hansen just as he saw Hoefer come out on the porch of the house, now remembering carrying his board up the rocks, remembering that that had been a high-tide day too with the outside reef pumping out at least a steady seven-foot with super hairy almost inside-out body-breaking rides, the last one sucking out so bad that sand off the bottom was coming up in the wall then everything exploding under him and after dragging himself in, body banged up, legs shaky going up the rocks, yet excited about the ride, there was Hansen, AWOL, sitting inside the car, a dark blue navy coat draped over his head covering his face; and, after sliding the board in the trunk, then getting in, saying hello, through the coat Hans said, "Hello, Chuck," and all the way into town neither moved nor said more and only when they reached the point and the old house had Gray seen Hansen's face and shaved slick as an egg, sunburned, peeling head (done by the screws at

Long Beach Naval Station Brig), a laughable contrast from his former full sunbleached blond surfer's natural . . .

"Sorry, man," Hoefer said, opening the door. He had his dark glasses on.

"What he'd say?"

"Nothing," putting the key in the ignition.

"He say anything about the syringe?"

"Nope," Hoefer said, looking in the side mirror. "I didn't push anything." Cars moved slowly across the glass. He started the engine.

"He's going to blow his mind up one of these days," Gray said.

"Well," Hoefer said, "maybe that's what he needs."

"Ha," Gray said, "you know he's a pretty good surfer when he wants to be."

"I haven't really watched him," Hoefer said.

"He's not as good as you but he's pretty, you know, I mean he has a good style, kind of like Mickey's."

There was an opening in the near lane and Hoefer let out the clutch, easing them into the traffic.

"You know," Gray said, "Deese has a kind of funny theory about Hans. Deese says everyone is born with a guardian angel, like, and he says Hans lost his a long time ago."

"Wow!" Hoefer laughed. He looked at Gray. Gray was grinning. Still laughing, Hoefer reached under the dash, clicking a plastic cartridge into the tape deck. Instantly, madrigal voices singing "Lucy in the Sky with Diamonds" filled the air.

"The Beatles are too much." Hoefer laughed, looking back at the road. The lane was open ahead and Hoefer shifted into second, then high, looking again over at Gray. Gray was slumped back, beating out the time on his thighs. Hoefer wondered who Gray's angel was.

"No," he said. He got up. She watched him chewing and swallowing, walking off. He forgot the check and came back. She pushed it to him. He looked at her.

"I'm coming," she said. "I'm the best man," he said. "I truly am. I truly love you." "I know you do," she said.

"You're not happy," he said. "Please, David," she said. She stood up, then walked on ahead.

He paid the check and they went outside. "God," he said, "I can't believe it. It just isn't true! It can't be true! Do you know what this means? Do you?" He started to cry. They walked along the long windows of the restaurant.

She started to touch him then didn't. "I know what you want," she said, "but I don't know if I can feel that way again."

"The truth," he said, "just tell me the truth."

"I really don't," she said. Then she said, "There is no truth."

"Jesus!" he said. "What is happening to me? I'm crying, for Christ's sakes. I'm goddamn crying!"

They were at the car. He opened her door. "You cried the time you asked for a divorce," she said, "the time right after you married me."

"I know," he said. "I remember. Here. Take the keys. I'm going to walk."

"No," she said, "don't be ridiculous."

"I can't stay where I'm not loved," he said. "I won't." He was looking down at the asphalt of the parking lot.

"No," she said bitterly, "I suppose not. I suppose you can't."

He looked up at her. "I can't," he said.

"Do what you want," she said. "You always have. Do anything. I'm tired. I'm going home."

He looked at her. She didn't move. He looked down at his shoes. "Good Christ," he said.

The Uses of the Past

She had long straight brown hair and a face like a child's, a gentle face. As they danced he told her she looked like his first wife, a beautiful girl. She seemed flattered and said that was nice and funny too because for some reason she felt like his first wife, like they were married.

When they left the bar they went home to her apartment. They shared a number she had and went to bed and for a moment he thought she was his first wife and said so but she didn't mind and told him to relax, just let things happen. He tried to and wanted to but he couldn't, it wasn't any use, her body wouldn't fit his, it wasn't the same.

Afterward she brought him a drink but he got up and dressed, saying he was sorry but he couldn't stay, did she mind, could he call her, he really did like her. She said yes, call anytime, and she wrote him out the number but he never did.

Thirty

"Do you think there's someone like that? I mean someone who would know how to be with me when they were with me? That's not being sentimental, is it? I mean someone who really wanted what I have to give. That's not too much to ask, is it? I mean they wouldn't have to stay or anything. I'm not silly enough to ask that. I mean I'm not the only woman in the world, am I. I certainly don't think that."

from

DIAMONDS

(1976)

Ho-Hum

She wouldn't get up in the mornings. He had had to make his own breakfast. She always took her mother's advice over his advice. It was her family always telling her what to do. She couldn't leave the house except for church, school, and Rainbow. That was how they got married. She had to get pregnant and she did. She always said she was glad about it. She always said she hated that house and she hated this town. She always said that, but both times when he had moved her away she would complain of loneliness and make him move her back. And that was really it, her always doing what her folks told her to do, the only one not telling him what to do was their little girl, age four, but she wanted to know why he wasn't at home. He wasn't at home because of the fighting, no hitting or that, just orneriness, angriness, constantly orneriness that made him too tired at work. And that was it, that was the main thing, a lot of his poor performance at work was the result of her not backing him up.

Now he didn't know what to do.

His wife still loved him, he knew she did, but earlier this morning he found evidence that a Terry Hammond, age twenty-two, had moved into the family house. He accused his wife of it but she denied it, saying only that a girlfriend had moved in, but said she was smoking marijuana now and, in general, just having a ball.

What he wanted to know was what he could do.

Was that sufficient grounds for custody?

Whitefolks

Besides, she had a good time up there, she felt free, really free. Why shouldn't she have? I told her that. What she did was not show up Friday and go on up with some guy she'd met the weekend before. She didn't come back till last night so you know who starts calling around, where is she, has anybody seen her. And all day yesterday he's over here, so concerned and all, so much the gentleman. And when she gets here and sees his car she can't make up her mind whether to come in or not because she knows she's going to get it. Well, he's so nice, treats her so nice, telling her he won't hit her, that he'll never ever hit her, that he won't even touch her unless she asks him to. Then comes the big pronouncement, he loves her, he says, he's finally realized he loves her. I get her in the kitchen and say that's bullshit and you know it, there's only one thing he loves and that's his old lady and two kids back in Chicago, that doesn't all the money you make go back there? That all you're doing is supporting some other chick and that chick can do anything she wants, but you, you can't even go on up to Frisco, that all that love shit he's giving you is just for Mom's sake so he can get you out of the house.

"And what's she say? Tells me to fuck off. Thinks I want him or something like that.

"Not that I'd mind, but the real thing is he doesn't like himself. 'Cause he's real light, right, all the darker blacks pick on him. So where does he fit in? You see what I mean? There's no way he can like himself. And if she likes him then what good is she? The only reason he wants her is because she makes him look good, but since he knows he's no good how can she be any good? That's why he's all the time pushing at her, all the time accusing her of coming on with these different guys she's out with, guys he sets her up with! Isn't that nuts? See what I mean?

"We've gotta work it so you can see them when they're out partying together, when she's not working. I mean, you won't believe it. Right at his side every second. Always looking up at him. Always nodding at everything he says. And does he watch her? She's locked! If she's got to pee she's got to ask! And he won't say a thing. Just keeps her waiting. I've seen him keep her as long as a couple of minutes, her sitting there all pinched-up looking with that little pinched-up smile on her face.

"It's just incredible! I'm just glad he doesn't like himself. He'd be just terrible if he did. You know how good-looking he is. He is really good-looking. He could get away with anything if he weren't such an asshole. I mean anything! I don't know anyone as good-looking as he is . . ."

I Tried My Best

S he fucked this spade dude, him saying, You know you need it, you know you do, you know you haven't been getting it right; a professional dancer and photographer from New York who said, Wow, who are you, I can't believe there's someone like you in a place like this; this big guy, a bearded cocaine dealer who wore Big Mac coveralls and drove a vw van, trying three times with him before deciding he was both a chauvinist and impotent; a younger guy from France, an architectural student at usc who lived in a terraced house in Topanga Canyon and who drove a Mercedes-Benz.

"We went camping and watched the sunset and, well, I've sort of gotten involved."

"That's nice," he said, a weak sick feeling starting to leak out into his voice. "I think that's good."

"It's not serious or anything, don't get the wrong idea, but I don't think I'm ready yet."

"Sure," he said.

"I think we should try this a while longer."

"All right," he said.

There was a silence.

"You'll call?"

"Sure," he said.

"Okay, I'm glad you called."

"All right," he said.

"I don't want you to take this too seriously. You won't, will you?"

"No," he said, "of course not."

"It isn't serious."

"All right," he said.

There was another silence.

"Well, I've got to go now," he said.

"All right. You call me now."

"I will," he said.

"You know I couldn't sleep at night after you left. I tried to be there. I did try."

"I know," he said.

"I tried my best."

"All right," he said. "G'bye."

"Bye."

He hung up the phone. The change kicked down and vibrated inside the box.

"What she have to tell me all that shit for?"

The Pecking Order

I n the eighth grade sixty-five boys tried out for the basketball team. John Beck, one of the shortest boys, survived Coach Wooten's first cut. That gave John hope.

Each night after practice for the next two weeks he walked home in the cold and dark, praying the same prayer:

Dear God, he prayed, please may I make the first fifteen; dear God, please may I make the first fifteen; dear, dear God, please may I make the first fifteen. He always stopped after the fifteenth repetition.

John made it through the second cut, and after practice on the day of the final cut, he was called into Coach Wooten's office.

"Beck," Coach Wooten said, "what am I going to do with you? You aren't tall and you aren't fast. I don't even know if you can shoot."

"I don't know, Coach," John said. "Does that mean I'm cut?"

"No," Coach Wooten said, "I'll tell you what. I'll let you stick it out on the practice squad. Maybe you can work your way into a few road games."

So John was on the squad as the seventeenth man. Twice Coach Wooten let him suit up for trips to other schools. He never let him suit up for a home game. John didn't log enough playing time for the felt letter he could wear on his athletic jacket.

That spring John decided he liked a pretty girl named Susan. He thought she was classy. The first time he walked her home he felt she wanted a kiss. He almost did, then he didn't. They had a date to go to a Y teen dance on Saturday. He thought he could kiss her then. When he went to her house on Saturday she wasn't ready to go. Her mother said she would be ready in a minute and went in the bedroom to talk to her. John could hear Susan crying in the bedroom. He didn't know why. A few minutes passed and Susan came out as if she hadn't been crying and they went to the dance. John had a good time at the dance and thought Susan did too. He didn't get a chance to kiss her but asked her out for the next Saturday. She said she couldn't. Later that week he asked her out again and she said to please not ask her.

Two years later, while a sophomore in high school, John began dating a girl named Karen, even though she wasn't one of the popular girls.

Five years later, one sunny spring day, John read *African Genesis*. He was now a sophomore in college and beginning to read on his own.

"The social order of the jackdaw," he read, "an extremely intelligent bird, indicates that a social animal does not only seek to dominate his fellows but the degree to which he succeeds obtains for him in the eyes of others his social ranking.

"Further," he read, "once established this ranking remains permanent throughout one's lifetime regardless of how early it was established in one's lifetime."

John couldn't believe what he had read. For three days, refusing all talk to leave his room, he lay in bed listening to rock 'n' roll on his radio.

A Classic Case

"A classic case, my doctor said, that's what he said I was. I stayed around my mother. My father was stern and distant, prone to violence. I spent all my time making female decisions. Doesn't that sound about right? They put me to work in the family business. A dead end. I couldn't be competitive with other males. Walking down the street I would imagine myself with breasts and hips, that I had a vagina, trying to confront it directly, telling my head to leave me alone, telling it to let me live. The more I fought it the worse it got. I started hearing whispers, from within and from without. Something had to be done. I couldn't go on. I had to be that which I was really to be. If I wasn't the one, I had to be the other. If all women were destructive, then why not take it up with guys? Become a screaming limp-wristed nelly queen. Certainly no more wife and Brentwood Country Club, house, furniture, and car. So I did. Quit. Walked out. Broke loose. Started the new life. Total disappointment! That wasn't me at all. Just another country club scene again but flopped over. The same games but in reverse. Even my doctor didn't know what to say. So on my own I started dropping those little psychic A-bombs in me, phoosss! Reprogramming the program. Fantastic! I remember it so clearly! The first time I dropped, just phoosss! You know. All the pain I thought was going to kill me, the revelations of self that would destroy me, were revealed as just my pain, pain from the inside, not the outside, that if I just rode with it I would live, nothing more than that pain was going to happen! I mean, I learned! Just accept your thoughts. Don't direct them. Don't take them into anything that is painful, don't take them into anything that is not. Your mind can take care of itself. It's a fantastic machine, and already knows everything it needs to know if you just let it alone. I mean that was beyond belief. I'd always been so damn busy worrying about what I should do, and the whole thing was just revelation, gospel, instant church. I must of dropped eight or nine times with nothing but good experiences, nothing in my head scaring me. So good-bye to Hollywood. That was the end of those scenes. I moved back over here. Got this job. Started building back up. Up from my instincts. Following the true me talking to myself. What you do is listen to yourself. You listen to yourself and get it surrounded with logic and take it out in the world. BAM! It gets blown to hell! Another lesson learned! Another defense changed! What's that change? Nothing! Nothing at all! You just take it from there. You're still you. I'm still me. I just charge right out into things now and see what happens. And that's me. I'm back. I've planted myself. When I was little I used to plant a garden. I loved to watch it grow. Now I've planted myself. It's tremendous. Like the other day I was talking with this woman who works with me and realized I was using the same kind of trip on her that I used to use to come on to guys with! Isn't that fantastic! I couldn't believe it!"

The Pursuit of Happiness

The first thing to do, he said, was never to get down on yourself, to always make things easy on yourself. If he became unhappy, he said, he always told himself to find out the cause, and then he changed it, no matter what the circumstances, it was always wrong to worry about the consequences.

Working at IBM taught him this. Right after Korea he had gone to work for IBM as a management trainee. His wife said if you hate it so much why don't you quit? He had been afraid to quit, but finally did, even though there wasn't another job to go to. To make ends meet he took work as a laborer hanging drywall. It turned out he liked this better, and it even paid more money. That was the first step, he said, but he still wasn't happy. Then he decided it wasn't what kind of job, it was having a boss. He decided to work for himself. He kept on drywalling but banked half of each paycheck. When the money was there he bought a new pickup and the tools and bid his first job, a subcontract to drywall six tract houses in West Covina. He won the bid, quit his job, and started his own business.

That was ten years ago.

It had been a tremendous step.

Right now his business was so good he was going into another business. The new business was so obvious a step it was hard to believe it hadn't been done, but it hadn't.

Metal-studding, he said, mass-produced wall-studding made of metal compounds. No more hammer and nails, no more wooden two-by-fours, no more slivers and splinters and mashed thumbs. All that would be needed would be an electric stapling gun and the studs. Houses would spring up in two days' time. First day, pour the foundation, slap in the studs. Second day, staple up the drywall and presto, instant house. Well, let the foundation cure first, so by second week, instant house. Two weeks tops.

As far as he knew, he said, he and his partner, a Malibu Colony psychiatrist, were the only men in the country working on it. They already had the patents secured, were building the first production machine. They had a building in La Puente where they would begin manufacturing, production to commence in the fall.

Right now they were testing different metals.

The studs would be made in various sizes from an amazing number of different compounds.

Their overall plan was franchise packaging.

By 1977 there would be metal-stud plants everywhere across the nation.

He wasn't rich now but by '77 he would be. By '77 metal studs would revolutionize the entire building industry, all benefits accruing back to him, and to his partner, of course.

And then it was on to Oregon.

By '77 he would be able to live anyplace he wanted and Oregon was the place. A man could live anywhere there and still go hunting and fishing. Or over in Idaho, the Snake River country, that was good country, live in a small town where everyone knew everybody.

Because that's what he wanted for his kids, he said, a nice small town. As a kid he had lived in a small town, which had made the difference. He hadn't had an old man. His old man had run off. There hadn't been any guidance and he got pretty wild. He would have gone to jail but his mother knew the judge and that got him off. He had a choice between the army or jail. Just having a choice made the difference.

People in a small town pull together, he said, you can't deny it.

If my two boys ever need it, he said, I want them to get the same kind of break I got, although, he said, he was doing everything in his power to make them feel wanted, not feeling wanted being the cause of most of the trouble in the world.

And that was the other advantage to living in a small town, because that was his other rule, that a man keep his own self-respect.

A man had to do that, he said. If he didn't, he was lost, and there wasn't a faster way to lose it than to have some woman cut you down.

Because I don't care who she is, he said, a woman will cheat on you, especially a pretty woman, but not in a small town, if the town was small enough, he said, a man could take off hunting or fishing and not have to worry, he would always know where his kids were and he would always know where his wife was, and what's more, his wife would know he knew and respect him for it, but L.A.?

You can have L.A., he said, too many people . . .

On Temple Street

En route with him to hear Maria Muldaur in concert, she rehearsed this basic speech, trying it out in several ways, but all the time underneath it wondering where the money was going to come from and what she could really do for a living:

"It's too bad you have to be you and I have to be me. I mean, that we've got to stand up here like this at each other, but fuck it, that's the way it is. I'm not taking any shit from you of any kind. But so what, right? Don't tell me what to do. Don't even think what the fuck I should do. Just worry about what you should do. You take care of you and I'll take care of me, and if you don't like it, shove it, either split or I'll split, it doesn't mean shit to me either way, though I don't want this to be hard on either one of us . . ."

Arts and Crafts

"Oh no . . . No, No . . . You just tell him, I mean, my God! I've already got Liza here, that's enough of a problem, isn't it! I mean I've already gone through it with him, that's just . . . Really! Like the water in the bathroom, he turns the water off in the bathroom, you go in to wash your hands and there's no water, there's no water in the toilet, he's turned it off with that little knob under the sink, or he takes a drawing and tears it in half, saying, So what, what difference does it make, it doesn't make any difference, all kinds of trips like that, some I can't even mention! My God! No . . . No one wants him here! I mean, I don't even know how to say this, a thing like this shouldn't even be said, but he laid this big trip on me about me being gay . . . Yes! I mean, I've had that happen before and hold it right there! . . . Right! He actually got out of his clothes, for God's sakes! And said, C'mon, do it to me. You're gay, aren't you? Sure you are! I had to practically demand that he stop! Don't do this, I said, this could be a very embarrassing thing! Very embarrassing! He had his pants dropped down right there on the floor, begging me for it! Pleading with me! I told him, You put those right back on! I mean, my God! . . . Yes! That's true! Really! I mean, it's not for me that I feel embarrassed, it's for him! I don't ever want to see him. No! Not ever! Not even walking by on the street! . . . Really!"

Bellflower Blvd.

He bought the Coke before they went in but when they went to open it there was no opener, he had had to pry the cap off against an iron corner of the bed frame and warm Coke blew out over everything, soaking the cover and blanket and sheets. She said she didn't mind, that she thought it was funny, but only wanted a sip, then went into the bathroom to clean herself. Standing there, looking at the mess they had made, he finished the rest by himself, then dressed, the Coke leaving a flat, dry, sticky taste in his mouth. Going out to the car, she was happy, then nervous, said she felt a little sick . . .

Around the Corner

She thought a revolution was going on and knew who was in it and how they were doing it. The first time we went to see her we couldn't. The orderly there told us she was heavily sedated and didn't want to see anyone. She thought she wasn't a person, he said, and thought no one else was one either.

A month later we still hadn't seen her but she was better and could talk over the telephone. The first thing she said was that it was nice there, really nice, that everyone there was nice too, well, almost everyone, but too monotone, everything was too, too monotone, way too monotone, that was why she was talking in a monotone voice, could we tell she was talking in a monotone voice? Then she said but she was reading again, reading all kinds of books, that there were so many kinds and she was going through it all very slowly, very, very slowly, and that was right, wasn't it, wasn't that right?

She called often after that, gradually becoming more vibrant, more excited about things, and on the first day after her release we all went for a drive and a walk, going up Sunset near the Whiskey to show her the new shops and to see who was playing.

We parked down Sunset from the Whiskey and walked up the street. She was very cheerful and bright, and I asked her if she wanted to go inside when we got there and get a drink, but she said no, she didn't want to go inside, she liked it outside, but she didn't like the smog.

Lea and I looked at each other. There wasn't any smog. The Santa Anas had been blowing all day and we both thought that's it, she's going out again, but we looked out across the city to see if we were wrong, and there was smog, a faint brownish haze barely visible behind the new skyscrapers over in Century City. We looked back to tell her she was right, but she wasn't there, wasn't anywhere on the sidewalk or over across the street.

"Oh, Christ," Lea said.

We hustled up the street, going past the Scientology offices, there was a parking lot with some cars in it, then the corner, and then there she was, standing partway up the sidewalk that continued up the hill, facing down an alleyway, looking toward an older building of dirty white stucco.

As we walked up to her, she shuddered. I looked at Lea. Lea didn't know either. We looked where she was looking. Inside a window was a darkened apartment, a stand-up lamp dimly on next to an old TV on against a back wall. I didn't know what she was seeing. Then back in the dark, sitting off to the side on a low couch, I saw two old women, both in housecoats, both very large, their legs out slack before them, facing the TV, its picture a dull, flickering blue.

"Oh, God," she said, "I know what they're doing . . ."

Pier Avenue

Dave's mother wasn't exactly stupid. Twice she got a bottle off me by giving me the key to her room in the Hermosa Biltmore and telling me to come up later, but both times the door was chained shut from the inside and she wouldn't answer. For obvious reasons I never told Dave about her and it became a source of amusement for me to watch her come to the door and give him the concerned mother routine of straightening his tie and pushing back his hair and then leave with a bottle of good Scotch that he would slip her. He claimed he kept track of the bottles she took but I never believed it. So much petty theft took place every day, with most of it happening during the day shift when Dave and I weren't working, that I assumed he marked the bottle off as stolen. However he covered it though, it seemed to work as Arnie, the owner, never complained. And if Dave's mother was using him to get free booze, I wasn't any better.

When I first went to work at the store I didn't know anyone in Hermosa, and Dave and I got along all right. He was just breaking up with his wife, Jo, and when he learned I was quits with my old lady he started taking a bottle for us and we would keep it under the counter and get tight together while we worked, which suited me just fine.

We started spending some free time together and several times spent the early part of the day shooting clay pigeons over in Palos Verdes. Dave was a hell of a shot, and something I'll never forget was the way he'd look over at me after he'd made a hard shot and say, "Christ, I'd like to have met Hemingway."

He wasn't kidding. As I got to know him better nearly all of our conversations would remind him of Hemingway. Dave had all the paperbacks by and on Hemingway and everything mentioned would be related to shooting and fishing or of going to the six-day bicycle races or boxing or bullfighting or Spain and Paris and Northern Michigan. Arnie said that one of the things that caused Jo to break with Dave was his obsession with Hemingway.

I could understand that. After a time the Hemingway talk started getting to me. I had already decided to quit the job as nothing in Hermosa was happening for me by then, and as I was making this decision I spent less and less time with Dave and finally stopped drinking at work with him. He didn't like it and stopped talking to me.

The last night I worked in the store, though, Dave opened a fifth of Black Label in a farewell gesture and said that one time some famous critic had gone to visit Hemingway and Hemingway had slammed a bottle down on the table and said, Goddamn it, if you're going to talk to me you're going to have a drink with me.

"Sure, Dave." I had to laugh. "I'll drink with you."

"Of course you will," he said.

And I took a drink.

I gave the bottle back to him, wiping the lip with the back of my hand, and he asked me where I was going to go. I said I didn't know right now but I didn't care so long as it was somewhere new.

He said he could understand that, he'd really like to do that too, but what he would really like to do would be to go to Africa.

"Well, why don't you?" I said.

"I can't," he said.

"Sure you can."

"No," he said, "I can't."

"If it's money why don't you quit and get a better job, then take off?"

"No," he said.

"Is it because of Jo?"

"No, it's simply convenient to work here."

"Bullshit," I said, "you're here because any minute you keep hoping Jo will sail in here and sit down on the magazine racks like she used to do."

"No, that's not true. It's my mother. I'm here because of my mother."

But he looked away as he said it and put the bottle down, and the next thing he did was grab his jacket and walk out the door.

That was the last time I saw him. We weren't very good friends to start with so I didn't mind that much, but he had been nice to me at a time when not many other people were and I was sorry I had opened my mouth.

Then last week by chance I was at a party in Palos Verdes Estates and looking down on the long sweep of South Bay I could see the Redondo and then the Hermosa Beach Pier. So in the morning I drove up the coast through Hermosa and stopped at the store.

Arnie was there and after a welcome he gave me Dave's new telephone number and told me to call him.

"I don't know about him," Arnie said. "He's still doing a good job here but he's into a new thing. You remember that Hemingway stuff?"

"For sure," I said.

"Well, it's space stuff now. He's saving his money to try to get into one of those space programs."

"That's something," I said.

"I don't know. You remember his apartment? All that skeet-shooting and deep-sea fishing gear? All that's gone now. He's got the whole thing fixed up like a spaceship. He's got this arm-chair he sits in, a big red job, with some kind of control panels built into the arms that control everything—windows, doors, the heat, lights, TV, the phone."

"Sounds like he's changed quite a bit," I said.

"I don't know," Arnie said. "I was talking to him the other day and he said what he likes about outer space is that it'll be a completely different place where a man has perfect control. He said if you land on a planet you don't like you simply get back in the ship and blast off. You think that sounds any different?"

"I don't know," I said.

"No different than crawling inside a bottle," Arnie said, "like a couple of characters I used to know."

"Sure, Arnie," I laughed, "but I'll never confess."

"Who was asking?" Arnie said.

I laughed again and went over to the phone. I dialed Dave's number and waited. The phone rang twice and then Dave's voice came on.

"Computer Center, Computer Control speaking."

"Dave," I said, "this is Dick. How are you?"

"Repeat, please."

"Norris," I said, "Dick Norris."

"Norris," Dave's voice said. "Norris, Dick. That does not compute."

"Hey, Dave . . ." I said.

"Repeat," the voice went on, "that does not compute."

The line went dead.

"Son of a bitch," I said. "He hung up on me."

"I told you." Arnie laughed, looking at me. "But I don't give a damn, so long as he does the job and comes to work on time."

"You're all heart, Arnie," I said.

"Isn't everyone?" Arnie said.

Blood

"A year ago I was divorced. I divorced on the advice of my father who said, Well, shit, get a divorce if that's the situation. We were sitting in a room in a hotel off L.A. International. We were on the seventh floor and I was bitterly complaining. My capacity for unhappiness was overwhelming. The misery of my complaints provoked my father. Divorce her, he repeated. I didn't have the money and told him so. He said he would pay for it. I sat there nodding my head. I wanted to punish my wife and divorce and abandonment seemed just. No doubt my old man knew what to do. I knew I didn't. He said to write him the amount I would need and he would wire it to me but under no circumstance was I to give my wife any of it. I agreed not to. Then he said a man was supposed to forgive the dead, wasn't he, that in time my wife would become as if dead to me and he hoped I could forgive her, he hoped that for me more than anything. I said I hoped so too, and he said it again, that I should forgive her, that it was the most important thing of all. If I didn't, he said, she would never go away, she wouldn't, she wouldn't. I looked up at him. There were tears in his eyes. Up here, he said. He was tapping the side of his head. I mean up here. Tears came to my eyes. Dad, I said. You have to, he said, you can't let them get the best of you, you can't let them do it . . ."

Paradise

As we walk by, a young girl steps out and hands us a pamphlet.

"Would you like to attend a meeting," she says, "a Buddhist meeting? It will show you the way to peace on the earth and self-enlightenment?"

"No, thank you," Lea said, "I already know the way."

"Ah, c'mon," the girl says, "you're putting me on . . ."

from

WILD CHERRIES

(1980)

Cut Flowers

"Sex works exactly the same way. Listen to this. I was going out with this gal, right, gorgeous, gorgeous gal, a client of mine. Well, I never laid a finger on her, never. Knew better than that. That's what everyone else would do. 'Cause she was fabulous. Totally. So we keep going out, getting to know each other better. I'm staying completely under control. It wasn't conscious on my part. Not completely. It was just what I was doing. So this one time she's over to pick me up. I'm in the bedroom fixing my tie. I turn around and there she is, sitting on the bed. I looked at her and said, What are you doing? We have a theater date in twenty minutes. Don't you want me? she says. Sure, babe, I said, absolutely, and we will, I mean, we both know that. Now c'mon, get off there, we've gotta get going.

"Okay. We go out a few more times. Same thing. I don't do a thing. So one night she's here. I'm sitting here, she's over there. So all of a sudden she just jumps across the couch and, well, so that was that.

"Now, okay; how does it end? Well, she ends it. She used to come over for the weekend. It was just great. She'd stay all weekend. We'd never go anywhere. We never went out for a minute. It was our refuge from the world. We didn't do much, make love, sometimes just cook, watch TV, maybe do some barbecue, make love some more. She never wore anything. All she'd wear would be one of my shirts. It was really fine. Just perfect. And she'd say I just loved you all weekend. Just was the key to the whole situation. I just loved you this weekend. Just was the way we wanted it. It was really good. Well, then she did it. She changed it. She said, I love you. I said, What are you saying? She said, I do, I love you. I just looked at her. She said, What's my future with you? I said, Babes, you just had your future with me.

"So that was it. I didn't see her again. Then about a year later she calls. She wants a couple of hundred dollars, she says. Something has gone wrong, see, and she knows she's not gonna make it. Sure, I tell her, c'mon over and pick it up. She comes over. I give her the money, but, like don't tell me what it's for, I tell her, just take it, you tell me what it's for and I might not approve. Okay, she says, and I could use another fifty for running money. Take a hundred, I tell her. No, fifty more was all she wanted.

"And that was it. I gave it to her and that was it, see. Because if you borrow money then I'm involved in your personal life, right? That's the way it is. I'm not a bank. I don't want your personal life. Only a bank can give you money and not be involved in your personal life. She knew that."

Bragging

The coat was folded lengthwise, and when he got in and laid it on my board I saw a rifle barrel emerge. He had a leather pack on the ground he had to squat to lift, and when he put it in back next to the coat I could smell blood. The pack was loaded with deer meat, 110 pounds of deer meat. He was Chet, he said, Chet the Jet of The Family Dog. He and his old lady had been with The Dog up in the Santa Lucias but she got pregnant, they'd moved down to Pacific Grove because of that. They were into macrobiotics but just brown rice wasn't giving her the strength, she wanted meat, so he'd gone back up there and shot a doe, good blood, sweet blood, graceful blood to put into a baby. He'd like to be back up there now. It was the only country. The National Guard was up there trying to run them out, that was federal land, but they couldn't find them. It was too rugged for helicopters, and The Dog had lookouts with walkie-talkies on the few roads in, that gave them a two-hour head start. They can't get us, he said. I knew you'd stop when I saw your car, he said.

Then he asked about my board, he liked its color.

"Aqua green," I said, "the color of clean winter surf. You know how a wave peaks over on itself, not breaking along all of its length at once, but peeling off down the line?"

I held up my hand, making a model of a breaking wave, curling the first two fingers to the base of my thumb, leaving the last two up.

"You interested in this?" I asked.

"Well," I said, "there's a pocket back under there, see, that's where you're trying to get, you sliding the board in, into the wall, its color going into the wave's color, you choosing the track, tracking yourself toward it, toward the setup, the wave sets itself up, goes vertical, the wall goes vertical, see, you thinking you won't make it, can't make it, the fin won't hold, can't hold, then bam, it's spilling over, the wave's spilling itself out and over, completely over, and suddenly you're there, the board has disappeared, it doesn't exist, it's just you moving fast on nothing, no sensation at all except light coming through the tunneling water enclosing you, you're there, completely inside, right inside the jewel, you've got it, the heart of the universe . . ."

"Like music," he said, "The Dog is into music. Like all the Avalon posters are Dog posters," he said. "Everything is worked out in a group. We all sit in a circle and get stoned and fire sentences at each other. The further out we go, the more people we get off. The ones that get everyone off we write down, the ones written down become the poster, the best combinations."

"Yeah," I said, "and then bam, it blows you out, it has to blow you out, there's trapped air in there, the wave has trapped air in behind you as it pours over, it has to blow it out, you blowing out with it."

And I went on, you use that speed to let you turn down the wave face, the speed from the drop giving you the juice to turn right back up into it again, see, the peak moving on down the line all this time, you organizing your attack again, playing variations on it, maybe going into it higher on the wall this time, this time sticking your arm into it, into the face to suck yourself back in even farther, deeper, trying to see how far in you can go and still make it out.

"Like music," he said, "just trying to get higher and higher. Just pour your mind at it and it opens up, right?"

"Yeah," I said, "that's it, that's where you want to live, that's where all the energy is. Some guys come out of there screaming," I said, "I mean they literally scream when they come out."

"That is far out," he said.

"Not everyone is into surfing that way, though. Most people just paddle out and get stoked if they get a ride."

He said he could understand that.

I said it's not something you can get right away, you have to work at it.

Like everything else, was his comment.

We rode in silence after that.

Coming into Pacific Grove he said he'd like to offer me a place to sleep but he hadn't seen his old lady in six days. I told him I didn't need a place to sleep.

He showed me where to turn, and we drove up a couple of blocks and stopped alongside a rusted Ford panel in gray primer coat, its left front hub resting on a wheel laid flat on the street.

He got out.

Beyond the panel was a two-story wood-frame house, white paint peeling off the sides, unpainted steps going up to a porch.

He reached in the back and pulled out the pack, then the coat with the rifle and said, "That's our place, take care now."

I watched him go across the lawn and up the stairs, then turn and wave and go inside.

I drove off up the street.

Sad Ending

He was going out with the younger girl when he took the older girl out. He had liked this girl for two years and knew she liked him but he didn't know what he wanted to do. Finally she said, I don't know about you, you're sleeping with the Hartley girl, aren't you, do you sleep with her? How about you, he said, you sleep with Muncy, don't you? She didn't answer right away. When it came, all she said was, Do you know what he tells me afterward, he tells me he loves me, he always tells me that.

And the ending with the younger girl was just the same.

He said it wasn't that he didn't love her, it was that he wanted to see other places and have other experiences first. She said, All right, and pulled him down to her. No, he said, it's the wrong time, you'll get pregnant. She didn't say anything, just sat up and dressed.

Whose Car Are We Riding In?

"That kind of talk makes me sick! I mean it! It does! I never took your power! If I took anything it's only because you gave it to me. People only take the power you give them. They can't take it from you! They can't! You're always talking about that, his power, her power. That's not important. 'Cause it's not! All you're talking about is your image, nothing else. That's all you're concerned about, how you look to others. You don't care about me. You don't. You don't want me to succeed in what I'm doing unless it's a compliment to you. Well, I don't care about that. Not anymore. If something bad happens to me I tell people about it. So what if they think I've lost something. We all lose something. There isn't anyone who doesn't. You'd just die if you thought people knew I talk to you this way, wouldn't you? You would. See what I mean? Yeah, you would."

Elko

"These are the songs: 'Hey, What Did the Blue Jay Say?'; 'Oh, My Goodness!'; 'Animal Crackers in My Soup'; 'At the Codfish Ball'; 'Polly Wolly Doodle'; 'On the Good Ship Lollipop.' Under his clothes he wore a bra and panties. When he got soaked with dishwater we could see them. He carried a hat to work but never wore it; he'd come in with snow on his hair, the hat inside his coat covering the cassette player. That player was his baby. No one knew where he was staying. Someone said one of the motels. We've got a big metal automatic that, once loaded, both washes and rinses all the plates. It takes about three minutes to cool down once it stops. You can't open it until then. While it cooled was when he'd play his tapes. Only Shirley Temple tapes. 'On the Good Ship Lollipop' was the one we would hear the most. It got so we knew all the words by heart and would make jokes with them. He never reacted to it. Everyone thought they knew why. As a joke someone said they thought he was from New York. Even though we made fun of him we tried to protect him. He always rejected it, though. He wasn't weak and he wasn't stupid. When he got killed no one knew who to contact. He was hit in the street after work. It was one in the morning and in the dark some drunken kids in a pickup slid on the snow through a red light and ran him over. When we came to work that morning we all went out in the street to see where it happened. There was nothing to show where he'd died. The plows had come early and pushed all the snow away. Dickie found a couple of black plastic pieces that probably were off the cassette player. He gave them to Charles. Charles took it the hardest. He tossed them in the trash. I got one of them out, a piece of gray plastic with an indent that probably was from one of the push buttons, and put it on top of the dishwasher. It sat there for a couple of weeks and then one morning when I came in it was gone."

Justice

"This guy got his money stolen and there weren't any lights there. It was an old joint, see, with only an electric bulb hanging out in the hall. He saw the guy go out of his room but only saw the back of his head. The cops came and asked for a description. He said, How the hell can I describe him, it was dark, I only saw the back of his head.

"Well, you know how a lineup works, it's always the guy in the middle that's guilty.

"So the cops got hold of some guy, threw him in the lineup, and told the guy that'd been robbed to make a positive on him.

"He said, How can I do that?

"They said, Just do it, we know it's him.

"So he went downtown and sat in there and the cops said, Just take our word for it.

"Well, you know how it is, all those lights shining on the suspects, you can see them but they can't see you. I was younger then and everyone older looked old to me, and this guy they had up there was about maybe forty, but just some poor old guy to me, he didn't look like much.

"Well? the cops said, and the guy who was to finger him says, No, I can't be sure, I don't know.

"That's him. Do it.

"No, he still wasn't going along with it, but they kept working on him and finally he says, Well, maybe it is.

"Do it, one of the cops says.

"When? the guy says.

"Now, this cop says.

"The man in the middle, the guy says.

"Louder, the cop says.

"So he says it again.

"And this poor old guy up there, he says, Mister you've got it wrong, I never robbed you, you're making a mistake.

"So the guy turns to the cops and says, I told you, what do I say now?

"Just repeat it.

"Well, he did, and the guy was made and sent to court and the judge gave him up to five and sent him to Quentin.

"Now it didn't seem right to me, but he was some guy they wanted to get so they got him. You know how it is, if they want you, they'll get you.

"Anyway, now it was my luck to be the one that had to drive him out to Quentin, me, and a cop named O'Brian. Now O'Brian was a square cop, he was on the straight, see, and I put it to him, I told him about it, that it didn't seem right to me.

"O'Brian listened to me and said, Well, the judge said he was guilty, didn't he?

"O'Brian wouldn't commit himself, see, but I still didn't think it was right and I said so.

"O'Brian didn't say anything, and we just took him out there, Knudson, I think his name was, and delivered him.

"Well, we're handing him over and while we're doing it O'Brian says to the guard, How's Hamilton doing? How's he been?

"Fine, the guard says.

"Can I talk to him? O'Brian says.

"Sure, Bill, the guard says. Whatever you want.

"That was his name, see, Bill, Bill O'Brian.

"So they called upstairs and had this Hamilton guy come down and O'Brian starts in talking with him, how's this, how's that, and so on. Well, this guy is in for rape, he's already done ten of it, and, Yes, everything's still the same, I'm still innocent, but it doesn't look like it's gonna do me any good. He's very polite about it, very gentlemanly, seems like a hell of a nice guy, and when we leave I tell O'Brian that, and O'Brian says, I know. Then he says, Listen, do you want to go downtown?

"Do I want to go downtown?

"I say, I don't know what you've got in mind, Bill, but that guy doesn't seem very guilty to me.

"I know, O'Brian says, and I'm going to get him out.

"So we go downtown and O'Brian pulls this guy's files and reads them over. I read along with him and when we're done I say, Bill, he sure seems all right to me.

"He does, O'Brian says, and he gets up and goes and calls a judge.

"Now this judge listens and says, What the hell, O'Brian, you're always sticking out for some guy who's not guilty.

"Well, read his record, O'Brian says, and tell me then.

"And that's what happened, he ordered the records over, read them, and freed the guy."

Baby

"Do you want a baby?"
"I don't know, do you?"
"I asked you."
"I do if you do."
"No, not yet. I'm not ready for that yet."
"All right, I'm not either."
"C'mere."
"No."
"C'mon!"
"No!"
"What the hell! One minute you're asking me if I want a baby and then the next you're cranky. Don't be so goddamn cranky."

"That's just the way I am. One minute I'm happy, the next I'm not."

What's to Be Done

"Going in the car I didn't think about it. I didn't start thinking about it until we'd already started running. Thinking isn't supposed to happen when you're in action, but that's not true. It isn't true at all. I'm thinking I don't like the way he shoots pool. Some guys when they shoot, they just don't win. They shoot good until the money shot, the eight-ball shot, then they choke. He's like that. Also, he won't say where he got the caps and crimpers, things you just can't buy! So there it is, I'm running my ass off, my heart up in my mouth, and that's what I'm thinking. I've told Tom what I think. He said, So what, man? What if he is? Our karma's too strong. What we're doing is right. Even if he is a snitch, no way he'll turn us over. But that's what I'm thinking when I hear it. I'm running like a son of a bitch and I hear it. I'm already off the fucking campus sprinting for the car and I hear it. First there's a thud, a really heavy thud, then a crackle, a long going-on-and-on crackle, then nothing, and I'm at the car scrambling to get in. Jesus Christ, Willy! John is yelling, We fucking did it! William! Tom is yelling at me. Eeeeeeeyow! he's yelling. Get this fucker going! I'm yelling. The car is already going. Eeeeeeeyow, Tom is yelling, we did it! We fucking did it! No shit! I'm yelling. John is pounding the seat. Willy, he yells, no shit! No fucking shit! I start yelling, too. Tom is driving like a son of a bitch."

So Long, John Wayne

They were married to different people but she got wet talking to him and he said, "Okay but afterward I won't be able to see you again."

No, that wasn't acceptable.

He said, "That's the way it is."

She said she didn't think so, but she was willing to take her chances with that.

He said, "No, I mean it," and he stopped it.

The next time they meet, it is by chance. Eight years have passed. They meet on a street in a larger town. She looks the same. He immediately thinks of that night. It excites him to think of it. He has remarried and so has she. She says, "We have some unfinished business." He can't believe it. "We do," he says, and he loves her for saying it, but as he stands there he starts remembering more of it, remembering bringing her inside, her lying down on the living room floor, her body literally going out of control on her, cramping on her, her moans embarrassing the hell out of him, him in the bedroom talking to his wife, the moans coming through the walls, him saying, No, no, nothing happened, she's just weird, is all, his wife saying, You did, didn't you, I know you did, if you didn't why would you even be in here saying anything, you'd be out there trying to help! Why don't you, you bastard, can't you finish what you've started, you can't, can you?

"But no," he says, "I'm flattered," he says, "but I really can't."

She smiles as he says this.

"I thought you'd say that," she says, "I could see it in your face, and I think that's amusing," she says, "because what you are is a male chauvinist pig, you realize that, and what's more this whole fucking town is full of men like you who think they're men, but they're not."

"A male chauvinist pig!" he says. "No," he laughs, "you're certainly wrong there."

She laughs too.

They stand there for a moment looking at each other.

Then she smiles at him and suddenly kisses him on the cheek.

"So long, John Wayne," she says, walking past him, "I've got to run."

"Hey!" he says to her, starting to go after her.

"No," she says back over her shoulder, "I really do have to run. Bye-bye."

Girls

"She wasn't yelling or anything, just running toward a group of hooches we'd set on fire, probably to get some kids out or something. A couple of kids ran out of one of the hooches, and there weren't any others so that was okay, we checked that, but she probably didn't know it, didn't know we'd checked it, so she just kept running even though we were yelling at her. The lieutenant told me to fire a burst over her head. I did, but she went down. I thought I'd missed her, all we wanted to do was have her stop, but when we went over and looked, I'd hit her, all right, she was lying facedown and the back of her head wasn't there.

"All I had to say at the court-martial was that I was ordered to fire over her head and thought I had, but I hit her, and I'm sick about it. They exonerated me, but out in the hall after it was over, one of the officers called me a dumb hick son of a bitch and said it was assholes like me that were ruining the Army.

"I do feel shitty about it, and I did it, it's there, there's nothing I can do about it, I killed other people there, I know that, but that doesn't bother me, that was exciting, I liked it, but I never knew for sure. I always wanted to. I thought I think I'll paint my bullets so when we count I'll know for sure it was me. I knew I had, see, so I really didn't have to know for sure, but this was different. I had a nice girl over there. At first I bought her, then she was just mine. It's hard getting used to American girls again. Everything they think goes right across their faces. You can see right through them.

"I don't know what I'm gonna do. That's what they always wanna know. Who the hell does? Some guys do, I guess. I had this one girl the other night. I'd picked her up on the beach and brought her over to the motel. I told you my car was broke down, didn't I? Well, I'd called my mom for help. I needed sixty bucks or so for some new pushrods, and instead of wiring it to me, since I'm in Seal Beach, she drives down right away. Well, I'm in there starting to get it on, right, and in she walks. She doesn't even knock! No shit! She just looks at us, turns around, and walks out! I had to go outside and catch her. She was really pissed. I had to laugh. She asked me what good was all this running around doing me? I said I didn't know. She said if I really wanted to be an actor, like I said, I should move back to L.A. and go to UCLA winter quarter, they've got the best acting school in the country. Use your GI Bill, she said. I don't know. Maybe I will. I don't know yet. It's a thought."

Welfare

"The universe isn't as mysterious as you think. Hidden laws no one has told you about eventually make themselves known. If, for example, twenty minutes before your second wedding, this one taking place in Oxnard, California, you stand outside the offices of the Justice of Peace and find yourself arguing with your wife-to-be as to whether or not she will be faithful and she says she can't say, she doesn't know, no one knows what the future holds, she can't say yes to something she doesn't know the answer to, you better conclude the argument with no yes, no marriage. If you don't, and she doesn't agree, the marriage then taking place, three years later here are three sentences you will hear: (1) 'Sex isn't that important'; (2) 'It's just another way of knowing someone'; (3) 'I don't know how to tell you this.'"

Power

"You can't be nice and give them that sweetness and candle-light talk. 'Cut the shit, man.' I love that. I love them. That look. Those high cheekbones. They'll cut you right off. You ignore them, you have to ignore them. The better-looking they are, the more you ignore them. You say, 'Who are you? What do you do anyway? I don't give a shit what you think. If I want to be nice to you I'll be nice to you. Fuck that. Fuck you.' Ah, they love that. They love power. All Scandinavian girls are like that. They go right for it. Sensitivity, no. Looks, no. But bust them, yes. Once you bust them, you've got them spread. It's true. You know how you've got them across your lap, you're moving them across your lap, and they get that hazy look in their eyes. Hmmmm, you know that look, ah, God, and they're the only ones, too, those blue, blue eyes, and you start to pull it out and they say, 'No, no, don't,' and their arms and legs go all steely around you, so you pull back and 'Pow, pow,' slap them right across the kisser, 'Don't tell me what to do, don't ever tell me what to do.' Ah, shit, man, they love it. You've got to do it that way. Then you've got them."

Beauty

"They think because they see it it's theirs. They're like that, all of them, that it's just there for them. They think it didn't exist before they saw it, that as soon as they see it they can put their hands on it, that it's theirs to put their hands on because they see it. They never can. The only ones that can are the ones that don't grab for it, the ones that lay back, and they only can if I decide they can. I certainly remember when the change came in me. I remember the exact moment. It was at a party. I couldn't get Paul to say anything. I don't mean at the party, I mean at any time. He would never talk to me. Not about anything. I tried all kinds of things to open him up. I was telling this woman I really respected about it, an older woman. I can't get that man to open up to me, I said. I said, I'd really like to get in his head for a while, to see what is really going on with him, to really know what he thinks. I said, I'd give anything to know what is going on with him. How old are you, she said, twenty-five? I said I was. She said, Yeah, that's about right. She said, Because I'm twenty-eight and there's no way I'm gonna be trying to find out what's in some man's head. If he can't open his mouth and tell me himself, she said, forget it, who needs it."

Wings and Soul

"I don't know," he said, "there might not be a damn thing left."

"Let's go see, huh, Weird?" he said to the cat.

Walking into the kitchen, he opened the refrigerator.

"Look at this."

It was completely empty.

"She took all the food, huh?" said Bruce. "She took all the furniture and she took all the food?"

"Well, let's eat out then," I said.

The cat was rubbing itself against Cliff's leg.

"Radical!" said Bruce.

"Naw," Cliff said, "it's too fucking late. What time does your plane leave?"

"Midnight," I said.

"Well, fuck. You'd think she'd at least leave something for poor ol' Weird. She loves the ol' Weirdster, you know."

Bruce and I laughed.

"Sure, Cliff," Bruce said to him.

"C'mere. I want you guys to see this."

He walked off toward the bathroom.

"Look at this. You haven't seen this." He was unwinding the bandage from his hand. A long, deep-looking cut, barely scabbed-over, curved across his palm.

"Jesus, Cliff!" I said.

"Not that. I mean this."

He snapped on the light.

It was blood. Blood on the walls. In long smears. More was on the tile over the tub. In splatters on the mirror over the sink.

Blood-soaked towels lay wadded up on the floor.

"Jesus Christ!" I said. "All that from your hand?"

"Yep."

"From that one cut?"

"That's it."

"She did that?"

"Unbelievable!" Bruce said. "She's a fucking maniac!"

"Isn't she," said Cliff.

"Take a look at this."

I was looking in the toilet. A gold wedding band lay motionless on the porcelain bottom of the bowl. It shone in the water.

"Was that in there this morning?"

"No," Cliff said.

He laughed.

"C'mon," Bruce told us, "let's get out of here."

"Suits me," I said.

"No."

Cliff was looking in the bowl.

"Nice touch, that girl."

I looked at him. His head was turned so I couldn't see his face.

"She must of come back while we were out picking you up at the airport."

"Well, let's go," Bruce said. "We'll make a night out of it. You can catch another flight, can't you?"

"Out having fun, was how she put it."

"For sure," I answered.

The cat appeared around the door. It looked at us, then turned and left.

"Fun."

"Well, let's go," Bruce said.

"No.

"No," he said again, looking up at us. He wasn't crying. I thought he had been, but he hadn't.

"You guys go on."

"Sure," I agreed, stepping past him.

"Listen," Bruce said, "she'll be back."

"No, Bruce," he answered, "no, she won't. That's a fucking stupid thing to say. I don't need that."

Bruce looked at him.

"I don't need it."

"Right," Bruce said. He stepped back. "It is. I apologize. You're right. That was really stupid."

"I hate her, you know. I hate her fucking guts! I'm the one that told her to go! To get her fucking ugly ass out of here! It was me!"

He turned away again.

This time he was crying.

We stood there watching him go through it.

"Listen," he said, "I'm really sorry I brought you guys here. I didn't mean to do this."

"Hey, Cliff," I said. "It's okay."

"I didn't," he said.

Apache Trails

Phillip,

When I was a girl, four years old, my mom gave a party and at some point late in the evening I was still awake (my dad was overseas) and a man came in my room and sat down on my bed. I don't remember the exact conversation, but he sat and talked with me, and he did something remarkable. He took a book and put it under my pillow. He told me to keep it there, that whenever I felt I wasn't a part of things, it wouldn't make any difference because I would have something of my own to do. All I had to do was take the book out and read it. I was too young then to know how to read, and he probably didn't know that, and I'm sure if he had he still wanted to plant that seed, and to this day I don't know who he was, but I do know the effect that had on me: I still believe people are understanding and compassionate.

And I assume that first about them.

Experience has shown me that other people weren't as lucky as that, and they distrust others first. And when they see compassion/niceness in people they think it's weakness.

I think you've made that mistake. You've seen my compassion as unsureness, my niceness as weakness.

I'm not saying this in any sentimental idea of us ever seeing each other again, but I do know that in the future when you meet someone, if you judge them as you did me, even if it is you that leaves first again, once more you'll be alone.

Gloria

Blue Skies

SPRING

I'm into making my room as visually attractive as possible. I buy old lace curtains and have plants. I do needlepoint. I was into the feminist thing for a time. I moved in with three other girls. Women should support other women. It's a rough world out there. But it was just a tight circle among them. It was a defeat. I certainly didn't expect that. And you don't get over defeat either. People say you do but you don't. Sure, you can rationalize it and say, Yes, I'm actually stronger at the broken place than I was before, but it isn't true. You don't get over it. You may be stronger at the broken place, but that just sets you up to get broken at some other place. So I moved out of there and now I'm living with three boys. They confuse me, too, but at least they're safe. I said to one, "Where are the men anymore?" and he said, "Where are the women?"

"A thing that intense has to burn out. I saw one of the last notes she left her: 'Sometimes I think you want more of me than there is to give.' I know if I saw someone looking into my eyes with that kind of intensity I'd be afraid. No one can meet that kind of need."

SUMMER

Ned, the island of Mykonos looks exactly like this. I live three minutes from this street. Life is primitive here—it is paradise! I live very cheap here. My baggage was stolen in Rome. So I am here for the summer. If you can, please write me: General Delivery, Mykonos Is., Greece. I rent a room for 3.00/a day, soon to move to a cheaper place. All the gay men in the world, I think, congregate in Mykonos—the influx begins now!

Love, Kitty

FALL

"Two people don't have to rot together. He showed me that. He and Ray don't. They give each other the freedom to be what they are. And that means if one has feelings that go somewhere else, then he has to be free to go somewhere else, then he's free to bring that experience back to the relationship. It's a pretty hard thing for most people to do. I'm really grateful to him for that. And I've had another insight. I'd been going out heavily. We'd all dress up and go out dancing. Studio One, the Unicorn, places like that. And I was sitting there watching everyone dance, and it suddenly occurred to me, No wonder I never meet anyone—how could I in these places? Not if you're female."

WINTER

Kit, I am writing this before we talk. What we talked about, I've been thinking about for a long time. So it wasn't a spur-of-the-moment decision. But, Kitten, really when I walked in this morning that was the end. But still never forget I'll miss you, and I love you very, very much. We've had a lot together. It won't end. This is only temporary, I hope. It's up to you also. I realize it takes two, but I can't take it anymore. There's a limit. But I just wanted you to know how much I really care. And how much thought it took to come to this. So, Kit, I hope you understand and still love me.

Forever, Julia

Come Home Please

"I just now realized I never asked you if you like the name I picked out for him. Which is quite selfish on my part. He is too much. He climbs up and down my ribs, chins himself now and then, then decides he is getting out of there and starts to dig a hole right in my side. Usually the left side. So then the right side of my tummy is completely flat and you can see him trying to push his way out of the left side until I can't stand it anymore and I move him to the center. This makes him very upset and he starts beating on my ribs and then on my tummy so I get sick. Like I said, if you were here I would undoubtedly take it out on you, the closest person, and you would hate me for being such a bitch. And I would hate you for thinking I was a bitch. Can't you see it all now, but wouldn't it be wonderful?"

Paradise Passing By

We're going in the room and Gail says, Grandma talks about passing over to the other side, she calls it the other side, she talks about people who are already there. We go over and look at her. Anne touches her arm. She is Anne's grandmother and she opens her eyes at the touch, but Gail keeps her from talking. Anne stands there looking down at her. The sheet is up under her chin and little pink cloth gloves are on her hands. All the flesh is gone from under her skin. She smiles at Anne then closes her eyes. A trickle of blood comes out her nose and lies in a bright smear across her lips. It isn't hemorrhage, it is blood from where she has rubbed her nostrils raw. That's what the gloves are for, Gail says, to keep her from opening the sores in her nose. I look at the gloves. Tiny dots of blood are bright on the tips of the pink fingers.

I look at her arm lying outside the sheet. It lies over a long, yellowish plastic tube extending out from under the sheet. The tube goes down into a large, opaque plastic jar on the floor. Fluid is running in the tube. The skin of her arm is silvery and reflects light. She says something. I look up. Gail is wiping off her mouth. Her eyes are open again.

"How are you?" Anne says.

She nods and closes her eyes.

"Is the pain bothering you? Do you want the doctor?"

"Are you going to move her up?"

It's the woman in the other bed.

"She was wanting to be cranked up before you came. If you move her up you'll need to call a nurse. You can't move anyone unless you have a nurse."

"I don't think so," Gail answers. "Thank you very much."

Grandma's eyes remain closed. Drops of sweat have broken out on her brow. She hasn't answered Anne's question. Her face under the fluorescent lighting is that of a tiny, old man. Gail begins wiping her brow. Anne bends and kisses her cheek. I touch her arm. The skin is warm and powdery, hanging off the bone. I squeeze her arm. Anne looks at me, indicating we should go. She looks back at Grandma. She bends to her again. I walk out into the hall. Gail comes out in a hurry, going by me down the hall for a doctor.

We're there the next night when she dies. Anne stands at her side, stroking her brow. Grandma lies in the same position as the night before, except this time her arms are folded across her chest and her head lies to the side on the pillow. The pink gloves are still on her hands. She hasn't opened her eyes once, and we know it's close. We've only just arrived, and we know it. I'm standing back against the wall by the door. I'm looking at Anne. Gail moves to take one of Grandma's hands.

For a second I look away, glancing up at the ceiling, and then I'm looking at Anne and Gail and at her, and something goes out of the room. That's all. One second I'm looking up, and then we're all looking at her and something goes out of the room.

The Fortunes of the Day

The next day not looking for her I saw her. I was doing laundry and there she was, outside, going by. I could let her walk past. It was up to me. I went out after her. She was stopped just past the window, looking at a notice put up by the ballet troupe class, her face wonderful looking, gray strands in her black hair, tan Boy Scout shirt, long Levi's skirt, beat-up Lady Canada boots.

I stepped around her, putting my hand on her side. She turned, looking up at me, not recognizing me. She looked stoned. Then she recognized me. I grabbed her and we hugged.

"What," she said, "what are you doing here?"

"Laundry," I said, "I'm doing laundry."

She laughed that same laugh.

"I'll help."

We turned and went back into the laundromat. My clothes were already dry and she helped me fold the shirts and T-shirts and jeans and then the sheets. I saw the fastest way to do it, started to do it, she was still figuring it out. "No," she said, "let's do it this way." I went along, feeling it made no difference. We folded the first one, then the others. We were finished and I put the box of fresh clothes under my arm.

"Well," she said, "don't forget your book."

I saw I had forgotten it.

She handed it to me.

Going outside together, I said nothing. We walked to the corner and she said, "I guess we can still have our life together, it's still there, there's a lot of time."

We stood there on the corner.

She said she had to find a bathroom, maybe into the Koffee Korral, but she didn't want to spend any more money.

She was looking up and down the Avenue.

I waited, looking at her.

She smiled, and put her face up gently for a kiss.

I hardly touched her, then thought I should have really kissed her.

The next day, though, having thought it through, I said, Like hell we can.

Then later in the week, just before I left town, we ran into each other again. We had some Chinese food at Shi-Shan's and she told me what was going on.

I didn't like what she was saying. The affairs she talked freely about were ones that were over with, and ugly to hear. The ones she hinted about were ones that weren't finished. I didn't want to listen. I just wanted to sit with her, something I'd never done, something she'd always wanted.

She wanted me to talk. She kept giving me openings. Finally she asked if I was still with my new girl.

I said, "Yes."

She didn't say anything, then, "Well, you still haven't said anything about yourself."

"No," I said.

"You just don't like to."

"No."

"You never did," she said, "not to outsiders."

"Outsiders," I said.

She was smiling.

"No, there isn't anything to say. We both know everything. Let's just sit here for a bit, okay?"

"But we can't, can we?"

"No," I said, "I guess not."

"I mean, we're not free to be here, are we?"

I looked at her.

"Well, I'm not sorry it happened."

"No," I said, "neither am I."

"I'm sorry," she said.

"Yes," I said, "I am too."

"You don't know what I went through. You have no idea."

"Well," I said, "I think—"

"You don't know. You don't. You know that ringing in your ears that you got? Well, I've got it now," she said. She kept on talking for a while then slowly stopped . . .

Faster Horses

" I 've dropped sixty at Golden Gate Fields. Hitchhiking back to San Anselmo it begins lightly raining. A cowboy in a silver Dodge work van picks me up outside San Quentin. I'm thinking now I'm down to thirty. He'd gone to the track once. He'd tapped out by the seventh. The guy that took him didn't want to leave until after the ninth. He told this guy he'd wait out in the car. He went out and after the ninth his friend comes out, breaks a two-by-four off one of the parking barricades, and starts in on the car with it. He'd jumped out, got hit, had his arm and jaw broke. He's lying on the ground, near unconsciousness, when the police arrive, arrest him, and book him for willful assault on private property before taking him to Emergency. The friend isn't arrested, saying, All I know is we both went broke but he left after the seventh and I just got out here. He musta gone crazy. At Bay Meadows, just before the end of the fall meet, leaning on the rail watching the horses being walked around in the saddling paddock before going out to post, the sixty-year-old man next to me, nicely dressed in a conservative gray suit and expensive-looking shoes, turns to me and quietly says, I lost it all, his face choked and sick. Hell, I tell him, it's all right. You'll make it back. No, he says, you don't understand. I lost it all, all of it, everything. That's what I'm thinking about while the cowboy tells me his story. Getting out in San Rafael, I start walking toward Fourth Street to hitch into San Anselmo. The only thing I can come up with to tell Carol is that I can't trade off, well, whatever it is, right, you know what I'm talking about, for love and rent any longer. Or else not say anything, just get my gear and adios it. Maybe it's just that easy. It probably is."

Friends

"You think she'll be back?"

"Sure. She had me drive all over hell looking for him before she took off."

"She did?"

"Sure."

"It's okay, then."

"Think so?"

"You're the one that thinks she'll be back."

"That's because she's freaked out. He's got the hammer on her. She's the one that says, 'Do you love me?' not him, then, 'I'm splitting,' and he says, 'Go,' and means it. Then it's her that writes and calls, not him."

"Well, he always takes her back."

"Not this time."

"Would you take her back? She's a lovely girl."

"No, she's not."

"What do you mean?"

"He won't take her back this time."

"Why?"

"Not after this morning."

"No!"

"Yes."

"You son of a bitch! You didn't!"

"I did."

"For real?"

"For real."

"And?"

"And what?"

"Marshall, you asshole! What about Marsh?"

"Marshall was being done a favor. He doesn't need a chick like that. No one needs a chick like that."

"You're a fool. She'll tell him."

"No, she won't."

"What if she does?"

"Then she does."

"She was just using you, man. To get back at him. To show him what she can do. She'll tell him, and he'll take her back."

"I don't think so, but even so, so what?"

"So you were just the patsy."

"So?"

"So you've lost a friend, man."

"Not really."

"Why not?"

"'Cause if that's what it takes to keep it together then they deserve each other. I don't need to know any people like that."

Speed Limit

I n 1958, when I was seventeen, I was seriously injured in a
nighttime truck accident, regaining consciousness on my
back out in a field, several older men around me, one trying to
get whiskey in my mouth.

No, I told him, my body has been crushed and I'm hemorrhaging inside, the alcohol will dilate the blood vessels and
speed the hemorrhaging, whiskey is the worst thing. Another
man, his arm supporting my head, was telling me an ambulance
would arrive soon.

I couldn't tell that I had pain, and I had seen my hips going
off to the right in a strange angle with the right leg ballooned
and turned wrong inside the pant leg and the right boot crushed
flat, but I had been rational enough to talk the man into taking
the whiskey bottle away so I knew my thinking was all right and,
no longer wanting to look at myself, I turned my head to my left,
looking out past the men into the darkness, and stopped thinking.

Where I was was in the Moses Lake desert. This is flat, desolate country of only some cheatgrass and low clumps of sage-
brush with no trees for miles in any direction save for back in
the town of Moses Lake. I knew that, and I knew my back must
be broken, and again there wasn't any pain, and my last thought
had been I hope I am not a paraplegic, and it was easy not to
think, and it didn't bother me that out there on the line where
the darkness of the land met the lighter darkness of the sky was
a stand of trees, large and dark, within an elliptical disc of a
strange, brilliant green, the green first flaring up about the boles,
moving up in bursts about the tops, then slowing, beginning to
flow out around all of the stand, etching each tree in exact loca-
tion, glowing about them with an intensity I could feel inside
me, then not moving, holding, as I knew that was where I was
going to go, and would.

And not telling the men what I was seeing, lying there watching that light breaking, then steadying itself about those trees, I thought, So this is how it happens, well, it's been a nice life, and only momentarily thought, No, it's too soon, knowing immediately that it wasn't, that for me it only went this far, that everything I was supposed to do was already done, and next awoke in an ambulance going at high speed toward Moses Lake and Moses Lake General Hospital.

Years later, in a truck stop garage in Flagstaff, Arizona, I talked with a trucker from Memphis, Tennessee, while an all-night mechanic worked on the heater of a car I was driving east to New York City.

This trucker, a large man in his late fifties, who introduced himself as Earl, had been in a Japanese POW camp on Luzon during 1942, '43, and '44. During his incarceration he contracted malaria and had it complicated by double pneumonia.

He should have died, he said, but for some miracle he didn't understand. He said due to the severity of the prison rations, as well as his illness, his body had been terribly racked by a lack of water. The crisis of the illness, he said, passed while he was hallucinating.

In his hallucination he knew he was dying and he was desperate for water. He said he found himself crawling in a field that was the slope of a hill. It was nighttime, and what was eerie was that the field was bathed in an unearthly yellowish light that came not from the sky but from the ground, and on the crest of the slope was a series of water spigots. He said he could see himself crawling in that yellow light toward those spigots and the water he absolutely had to have. He said he crawled and crawled and almost reached one of the spigots. He said he was very glad he hadn't because he knew if he had, that the moment he tasted that water he would be dead.

I thought his story was remarkable and told him my story, pointing out the similarity of the eerie lights, and the fact that dying seemed to be a peaceful journey to a new place.

He said, Perhaps, but he didn't think so. He said from his experience it had been terrifying.

I said in my experience it had not.

He said, Well, and then told me how to drive across country the fastest way: by getting behind any semi that has an antenna on top of each of the outside rearview mirrors. Go fast when he goes fast, he said, and slow down when he does; those antennas mean he is two-way radio equipped and has all the latest information within at least a forty-to-sixty-mile radius of where all the police and speed traps are.

I thanked him warmly.

We shook hands and he left.

Main Switch

"Mickey, he's so funny, he thinks he's so hot! He comes over in the afternoon and sets there pulling at himself saying, Doesn't that excite you, it excites the hell out of me, I know it excites you. I'll say, God, Mickey, don't be so crude! He thinks he's got so much going for him! He says women are simply mad about his body, they crave it all the time. I say, Hell, Mickey, that's no big deal, women crave lots of guys' bodies, sex isn't abnormal, you know, everybody does it. He's got a white Cadillac. When he first got it he took me outside to look at it. Look at this, baby, he says, I bought it just for us. Look at the size of that backseat. Righteous, huh?

Sure, Mickey, I say, you and some other chick get in back there and I'll drive you guys around. But, damn, he is good, you know. He's rough. And I like it. I like a guy who just grabs you and takes over. But then I want someone who's nice, too. I guess I want it all. I've got this other guy who's nuts about me, but he's all moony about it, his brain is just mush. He's something else. He wants me to come live with him. I think about it. 'Cause Mickey really isn't that hot. All the girls that're crazy about him are fat. Real fat. He doesn't pick any foxes. So, of course they're nuts about

"We were together three and a half years. I kept asking her to marry me. She said, No, ask me some time when you're serious! What the hell, I was serious! Then one day for no reason she decides she wants to live alone. Why? I ask her. It feels too close, she says. She thinks about me too much, she says, it takes too much of her time. What the hell, you know! Women are weird, they don't know what the fuck they want. It wasn't another guy, she said. I thought it was. So, anyway, I drove her down to Long Beach, her family and friends are there. So there I am in a strange town, eighty bucks in my pocket, no job, him. He can only have a girl once, he says. Once he's had her, it's all over, she doesn't turn him on. A new chick a night, he says. He's funny, all right. He's fun to kid around with."

no place to live. I know I can't stay there 'cause it's her town, right, so I drive along the coast and end up here in the same fix, no job, no place to live, knowing no one, and even less money. Me and my dog slept in the van for a month, scuffling around, trying to get up enough money for a place to rent. Then I met Ted here and started working steady. Man, you don't know how to relate to chicks, you know, you've been out of circulation so long you don't know what to say to them. So I start going out and it starts coming back. And then about six months later, man, I'm doing good, got a hot new lady, a place, a few bucks in my pocket, things are looking up and bang, there's a knock on my door! Out of the blue! It's her! She wants to come back. Well, I don't know, I'm not missing her so much, you know, I'm not so sure I want her back, but I let her in. She gets knocked up right away. We get married and now we've got a little son. It's weird, but it seems like when you want them they don't want anything to do with you, they only want you when you don't want them. And another thing I've noticed, if you really want to score just slip a wedding band on. You wouldn't believe the number of times I've been propositioned since we've gotten married. It never happened before. Right here at work, man, in this garage. Women are doing that to me all the time now."

Romance

We used to see them in the District when all the small-time dealers were working psychedelics on the Avenue. You would be sitting in the Hasty Tasty having a late-night coffee and you would see them glide by the windows like a ballet of luminous spectra. And sometimes their appearance would upset people.

One night a young, long-haired guy in a leather coat stood up and challenged them. They had just come in, and this guy said, "Why do you do that?" He had been sitting down, relaxed, before they came in.

"Do what?" the white-faced guy nearest him said.

"Put that crap on your faces?"

"What crap? What's wrong with my face?"

"The white stuff," the longhair said.

"White stuff? What white stuff?"

"Ah, shit," the longhair said. He sat down and stumbled.

They laughed.

"You're all ridiculous," the longhair said.

"No," a girl seated at a table in the corner said, "you've all been to a party, right?"

"No," said the Botticelli-looking girl of the two white-faced girls, "we're out exploring, you see." Her smile was genuine under the dusty white of her face, and I thought, Ah, Christ, look at her. She was right out of *Children of Paradise*, 1900 Paris, her beauty as precise and ethereal as that of the film, but one going even further back than that, past classical film, classical painting, past all education.

"Ah, you're all fucked up is what you are," the longhair said. He was standing up again.

All four of the white-faced people laughed and turned away, looking for a table of their own. The long-haired guy sat down again.

That was not an unusual response. They nearly always caused some kind of response, and you never knew what direction it would take.

The last time I saw them was several months later. It was the Hasty Tasty again. They came in and went into the back. I took my coffee to a table by theirs. The Botticelli-faced girl was telling the other white-faced girl a simple thing about eye contact. She was looking back and forth at me, her green eyes constantly checking when I looked back into them.

"One of the first things private detectives learn when they are assigned to tail someone," she said, "is to never establish eye contact, eye contact unsettles the soul, you make eye contact with a man on the street and he thinks you desire him, or," she said, "if you're a male, and make eye contact with an older woman she'll feel flattered, think rape, and hurry away clutching her purse tightly against herself. Can you see me as an older woman clutching my purse to me?"

She was looking at me as she said this, and she stood up and pantomimed scurrying out the door.

It was a few seconds before I, along with everyone else, realized what had happened.

She was gone.

Then the other three got up, and went out after her, all of them looking very happy.

Harrah's Club

"Heart attack at forty, a massive one. Then a second one. Hell, it was the first one that damn near got me. Now it's atrial fibrillation. I get that. You know what that is? Your heart skips. It beats without rhythm. I'm living on pills. Heart pills. Blood pills. Nerve pills. I did it to myself, too. No one else. I decided the only thing in life was money and went right for it. And I got it, too. First as a service manager for Toyota, and then with my own agency. Worked twice as many hours as I should have. Drank. Smoked. Did coke. Yeah, that's right, did coke and dropped like a rock right on the showroom floor. Right on the floor. The second one I spent ninety hospital days on. They had to operate twice. I threw off some clots and they had to go in and get the clots and a fucking staph infection set in in the incision. Isn't that the way? Yeah, well, it gets pretty damn rough sometimes. 'Cause I just get out and over that and then my wife took it. Went into a coma. Comatose thirty days, then she went, tumor under the brain. That's why they couldn't find it, they said. They couldn't see it. *Under* the brain. So what can you do? Nothing. Not a goddamn thing. You just get over one thing and something else goes. Sometimes it gets me. We had a lot of plans. There was nothing wrong with her. We both agreed I had to slow down and do something else. It was headed that way. We'd finally worked a lot of things out. Nothing wrong with her. Nothing at all. So what can you do? The kids pretty much have lives of their own. They seem to forget about poor old Dad. I set the oldest one up in business, too. They're good kids, though. Can't blame them. I wasn't any different myself at their age. Who does care about old Dad? Ah, what the hell. I don't know. I really don't. I don't know one good reason why I'm still here. It's already over. Some goddamn primitive instinct to survive, I guess. Hell, that's all the past, isn't it. You can't think about that crap. You do, you might as well go upstairs and get it over with."

How It's Done

"Yes, sure, he doesn't challenge, he just sits and listens. He's just easy to be around. And when I talk, if what I say doesn't make sense, well, it just collapses away on its own. And he doesn't *not* understand. Because if it's a true thought, he *laughs*. I really love his laugh. Did I tell you how we got started? He took me to Olympia and to the hotel downtown and then upstairs after we ate. It was the nicest room they had there, and he sat me in this big velvet overstuffed chair and listened to me the rest of the afternoon, never once trying anything sexual. It was snowing outside, you know, and I talked and talked and then we watched some TV and got in bed together and went to sleep. Isn't that nice?"

Immaculate Conception

"I've blown it, I know I have, I've shown you, I've told you, I feel love when I see you're stronger, you make me love you when I see you're stronger, you do and I hate it, I want to wreck it, I can't stand it, I do, I want you to want me, that's how I know I've lost."

EMPTY POCKETS

AND OTHER STORIES

Dear Anthony

Dear Anthony,

Anthony, I am tired of this bullshit between you and Angela Ramirez. Thursday when I came to school people was telling me you are still talking to her and in the bathroom it says I Love Anthony Washington in big black letters and when you are walking out it says ANGELA RAMIREZ—XO—ANTHONY WASHINGTON.

Anthony, I really don't know what to do about you. Then your ass gets all mad when I'm with Aaron or talking on the phone to him. I hope you have a lot of fun with Angela because she doesn't do the things I do. And you know what I mean. I hope she makes you very happy, even though I don't because I keep on making you mad all the time.

Anthony, if you do like her let me know now, I don't want to find out from someone else, I want to see your face when you say it.

So has she asked you to go to Grad Night with her? If you aren't still talking to her, or going with her like you say, why is everyone talking you are, or are they trying to matchmake?

Anthony, how do you think I feel when they are telling me this shit? You think I am just going to let it slip on past? Is that who you gave my bunny rabbit to? Because I don't have it. Or is it at the store like you said?

Anthony, the reason why you didn't get this letter a long time ago was because I wasn't finished writing it. If I was, you would have got it a hell of a long time ago. The reason why I crossed out your and Angela's name in the bathroom was because I like you too damned much. That's why I crossed it out.

And I guess I should stop coming over to your house when your folks are gone, stop calling you, and stop having you know what I mean with you.

And nothing is going on between me and Aaron Robinson, no matter what you say! That's all I have to say! And I am going to stop liking you! You don't think I can, but you are in for a great big surprise! Well, I am about to end writing this. I will probably talk to you later.

Love Always,

Me

The Prowler

Michael folded the rug over and pushed it up against the door. He had the bed already made, the pillows shaped like a body under the quilt. He came back and got up on the bed and carefully opened his window. It didn't make any noise. He held still and listened. He didn't hear anything.

He stepped up on the bed, then slid his body out the opening. Turning back around, he eased the window down, and listened.

Crickets droned from somewhere in the backyard. He could smell his mother's jasmine. His Ford sat mute next to his mom's vw and his dad's Chevy.

He walked to the bicycle leaning against the carport post and pushed it down the driveway and walked it, going left up the nighttime street.

The houses along both sides of the street were all dark with only the Keplar's bedroom lights on.

Viola Keplar was his mom's best friend and very weird.

One afternoon she had come out of her house in a bathrobe just as Michael was coming home from school. As he got out of his car she called him over and asked him what she should do about her husband. Michael had said, "Excuse me?" She said, "I was told you had the highest IQ in the high school so I thought maybe you could help me figure out what to do."

Her bathrobe had been partially open and he saw a rounded curve of her breast that was definitely bigger than Beverly's, and he didn't know what she wanted, so he said, "I don't know how I could help you," and thinking about it now he thought about Gunderson whose thirty-year-old neighbor was sleeping with him every noon hour, or so Gunner said, which was at least partially true, true that she was sleeping with Gunner, but was that what Vi Keplar had in mind? And the real truth was that he and Beverly had not really had sex, had sexual intercourse, and Vi Keplar scared him.

Michael wondered what Vi Keplar was doing behind that lighted window. Don Keplar's car was home. He was probably in the bedroom with her. Of course he was.

Then Michael was past their house, and he got on the bike and began riding down Winnebago toward Modoc and on Modoc turned left toward town. Beverly was babysitting the Monahan kids on Cherokee Street and by going down Modoc at this time of night there was far less chance of anyone seeing him.

So far there had been no cars. He looked at his watch again. Ten minutes past one. The night air was cool. The bike moved silently. Headlights appeared down the street and Michael quickly turned up a driveway and got off by the parked car and waited until the car passed by. A dog started barking two houses over.

Michael got back on the bike and rode it out onto the street and headed toward Cherokee. Beverly's dad, Glenn, was known to drive by and check on her when she was babysitting, sometimes sitting inside his big Buick down the street, watching. The sound of the barking faded away. Then Michael was turning left along Cherokee and he didn't see any cars parked where they shouldn't be. The Monahans had a nice cat that Michael liked. The cat was very friendly to Michael and would always appear when Michael showed up. It was a gray-and-black-striped cat with yellow eyes and would arch its back when Michael rubbed the fur on top of its head right above its eyes. He wondered if it would show up tonight.

Michael coasted up the driveway, dismounted, and walked the bike into the shadows at the back of the house and placed the bike there.

He heard the cat purring at his feet and he reached down and picked her up. She lifted easily, and he cradled her with his left arm crossed along his stomach and rubbed her head and neck with his right hand walking her along the back of the house to the sliding glass doors that opened onto the brick patio and the backyard.

The cat was purring heavily when Beverly came to the door and opened it.

"I didn't think you were coming," she said.

"I had to make sure that my folks were asleep."

"Well, it's really late," she said, "and I don't know what time they're coming home. They could be here any minute."

"I love this cat," Michael said. He put the cat down.

Beverly took his hand and led him through the kitchen into the living room.

"What do you want to do? Should we watch TV?"

"I don't know," Michael said. "What were you doing before I arrived?"

"Sleeping," Beverly said. "I tried staying awake, but I fell asleep. I don't know what woke me up."

"Maybe it was the cat," Michael said. "When did you let her out?"

"Just before I went to sleep, I guess."

"C'mere," Michael said, and he put his arms around her and she stepped into them and put her head on his chest, and then turned her face up for a kiss. It was a good, long kiss with his tongue going into her mouth and her lips firm and wet against his, and he felt her tongue going into his mouth and he started getting really excited and he felt himself getting hard and they sat down on the couch and the cat jumped up on the arm of the couch and Michael felt it brush itself against the back of his neck and then it was gone and his hands were up inside Beverly's shirt and he was cupping her breasts and getting even more excited, girls were so wonderful and so strange, how they were built, how they felt and tasted and smelled, so different, and yet so familiar, and she helped him undo her brassiere, and lifted her shirt and pulled her bra off and offered her left breast to him while she guided his mouth to it with her fingers pulling his head lightly down to it and then it was in his mouth and he thought he was going to come and he pulled back.

"What's wrong?" she said.

"Nothing," Michael said. "Let me just take a minute."

"No!" she laughed, and she pulled him to her again and Michael said, "No, wait for a minute," and he reached over and turned the floor lamp off so the only light in the room was coming from the light left on in the kitchen, and this time when he put his mouth on her breast he unsnapped his jeans and let his cock come out and she put her hand on it and touched it and slowly pulled on it and he lifted her skirt up and pulled her underwear down and she laid back on the couch and let him pull the underwear off along both legs over her shoes and she kept holding on to him and pulled on him and then he was lying on top of her and slowly rubbing himself back and forth on her and they were kissing and he felt something stopping him and she winced and he pushed again and said, "Am I in?" And Beverly said, "No, I don't think so."

"No?"

"Maybe," Beverly said. "I don't know. I don't think so, but I'm not sure."

"I'll go slow," Michael said.

"I don't know. Maybe we shouldn't," she said.

Michael had not yet ever been inside a girl, and this would be the first time for Beverly, too, and he lay still against her for a moment in the dark, feeling her heart beating and her breathing, and then he heard the cat meow and meow again and then car headlights swept into the driveway outside and Beverly said, "Oh, my God!" and was pushing him off, and Michael said, "Jesus!" and she was sitting up and then scrambling on the floor for her underwear and he grabbed his jeans, pulling them up, and she said, "Hurry, Michael, hurry! Go out the back. They'll come in the front door and it's locked."

Michael was already moving, and going into the kitchen he saw the car lights go out and heard the car door open and slam shut and he waited by the back door until he heard the other car door open and shut with the footsteps going away on the concrete toward the front of the house.

As he slid the door open the cat came outside with him and he silently tried to put her back inside but she wouldn't go. He slid the door closed and waited. The cat was rubbing herself back and forth on his leg and he heard them go inside the house and saw the light from the living room go on and he waited another moment, his heart still beating really fast, and whispered, "I've got to go," to the cat.

He got the bike and wheeled it down the side of the house along the Monahan's Chrysler and got on and started pedaling back up the street.

The cat, running on the side of the street along the other houses, darting in and out among the shrubbery, followed him for several blocks and then she was gone.

Michael was pedaling now as fast as he could get the bike to go. Everything was dark out and he felt safe. His only worry now was getting home unseen, then getting inside without waking anyone. But what if his mom had already come in to check on him and had discovered the pillows under the covers? Or his dad had?

Well, he would know in a few minutes. He really hoped they hadn't.

He was sweating under his arms and sweat broke out on his forehead now, and he pushed hard, the bike flying, and by Paul Hayes's house the automatic lawn sprinklers went on, shooting spray out across the grass and into the street. Michael rode through the showers, the little drops hitting his face and neck and arms, and then he came off Modoc and turned down Winnebago, all the lights of the houses still out except for the Keplar's bedroom window, and then it went out just as Michael approached, and he coasted on the bike, not wanting them to hear him.

Then, for some reason, not knowing why he was doing it, he let the bike slow, and dropped it on the grass right by the curb and walked up to the bedroom window.

There was a curtain across it, and stepping up to the sill he pressed his ear to the glass and tried to listen. Someone was saying something, but it was too hard to hear, and then there was nothing, and then, just as Michael started to step back, he heard Don Keplar say, "Say *I am fucking*. Say it. Say *I am fucking*." And then Vi Keplar said, "I am fucking."

"Say it again," Don Keplar said.

"I am fucking," Vi Keplar said. Her voice had gasps of air in it.
Michael was stunned.

He pulled away from the glass. He couldn't believe it. He
pressed his ear against the glass again. This time there was nothing. He couldn't hear anything. He stayed there a moment longer. Then he turned and banged into a garbage can.

Michael took off out onto the lawn, grabbed up his bike and
ran across the street with it. Moving into the carport he saw his
dad's Chevy was gone. Oh, Jesus, he thought, he's gone out to
look for me.

A car went by on the street, headlights flaring. It was a black
four-door Oldsmobile, not anyone's car he knew. The street
went quiet, the sound of the car vanishing. Michael laid the bike
up against the post, then walked around back to his window.
He waited and listened. The crickets were working. The smell
of jasmine was strong. He slid the window up. The rug was still
pushed up against the door. No one had looked in, thank God.

He boosted himself up and slid in on his stomach and got
down on the bed and waited until his breathing calmed down.
Where had his dad gone? He undressed and tossed his clothes
on the floor and got into bed and lay there for quite a while,
thinking about his dad and how there was no way he would
know that he, Michael, had gone out, and about Beverly and
what she must have said, if she had got caught or not, and then
about Vi Keplar and Don Keplar and how somehow that made
it all sound dirty, really dirty, and how with Beverly it didn't feel
like that at all, and if he and Beverly had really done it yet, had
really achieved the sensation of having arrived on the planet, as
Gunner had put it, and he was really glad he really didn't know
Vi Keplar and how she was, not at all, and that Beverly was
going to be babysitting at the Monahan's for at least two more
nights this week since both of the Monahans were working out
at the county fair, and that he would have to sneak out of the
house much earlier than he had tonight. He could do that. He
knew he would do that.

Then it was late in the morning, and when he got up and went into the kitchen his mom was there mixing up pancake batter, and she said, "Good morning, sleepyhead."

"Where's Dad?" Michael said.

"I don't know," his mom said. "You want some pancakes?"

"Sure."

"Would you get out the milk? I need a little more here."

Michael went over to the refrigerator and took out the milk.

"You know what, Mom?" Michael said. "I'd like to get a cat."

"A cat?"

"Yes."

"What would you do with a cat? You're going off to college soon enough. Who would take care of it then, me? No, thank you."

"Cats take care of themselves."

"Oh, brother," his mom said.

The phone rang and his mom answered it.

Michael brought the milk over to the counter and set it down next to the bowl. His mom was listening on the phone.

"Really! That's terrible!" she said. She listened for a few moments, then said, "No, come on over. I really want to hear this."

She hung up the phone.

"Who was that?" Michael said.

"Vi. She's coming over for a coffee. They had a prowler last night."

She picked up the milk and poured a little into the bowl.

"They did?" Michael said.

"I guess so. Don heard something outside and went out to look and he saw a car going away down the street."

"What kind of car?"

"I don't know. She said a black car."

"That's scary," Michael said.

"You just never know," his mom said, stirring the batter.

"You know what, Mom?" Michael said. "I'm going to skip breakfast. I've got to get going."

"Where are you going?"

"Over to Gunner's. We're going over to Richland today to look at some cars."

"What's wrong with the car you've got?"

"Nothing's wrong with the car I've got. We just like to look at cars."

"Well, you should wait and hear what Vi has to say. If she describes the car Don saw maybe you'll know whose it is."

"I don't think so, Mom. If this is about the pancakes, it's all right. I'm just not hungry. Thank you anyway. I'll let you make them for me tomorrow."

"Well, aren't I the lucky one," his mother said with a laugh. "Go on. Get out of here."

Michael turned to go.

"About the cat," his mother said. "You'll have to ask your father."

"He won't care," Michael said. "He's never here."

He hadn't been looking at his mom when he said this and now as he did, he saw her face had broken. A bad feeling, blinding him to the space around them, flooded out into the room, his mother standing there in the middle of the darkness of it.

"I'm sorry, Mom," Michael said.

"You don't know how hard it is," his mother said. "You don't know how hard I try to keep things the same for you. Things aren't the same. I can't do it anymore."

She broke out crying.

"I am so sorry, Mom." He was stepping to her.

"Go on. Get out of here," his mother said. "I need to compose myself before Vi gets here. If you want a cat you should get one. Who am I to say you shouldn't?"

"Jeez, Mom," Michael said. "I am really sorry. Come here."

Michael put his arms around his mom. Her shoulders felt so thin.

Chimes rang through the house.

"That's Vi," his mom said.

"What am I going to do?" his mom said.

She wasn't talking about Vi.

"I don't know," Michael said.

Claire

"I must tell you a love story. This will be a love story, my love story for you. It's about Brian, and how it ended for me with Brian. You remember he and Lola were married then? He was seeing me and it became, well, it became too involved, too intense, he was so demanding, so needy, he needed me to fix things so much it wasn't for me, so I ended it. I ended it, and then right after, I ran into Lola in Smiley's, and she was very drunk. She was very drunk and she came up to me saying, 'I know what you've been doing, I know, and I'm going to beat you up.' I said. 'What is this? Yes, it's true, but you're too late, it's already over, it's finished, I've ended it with him.' Now she was very, very drunk, so it ended up that I had to drive her home and put her to bed. Since I had to do that and it was raining I couldn't walk home. It was her car, you see, I didn't own a car then, so I had to stay over, and we slept together in her bed, and I made love with her. It was very funny. I'm wearing Brian's clothes, his robe, and I play Brian's role with her, and in the morning she says, 'My God, what did we do?' And I said, 'I don't know. What do you mean?' And she says, 'Brian. What are we going to do about Brian?' And I said, 'I don't know. What do you want me to do? Do you want me to tell him? Is that it?' So when Brian came in she told him, you see, and that is my love story for you this evening."

Gone to Polyester

The waitress was forty years old. Wore her hair piled up on top her head. Unfolded the linen napkin and put it on the boy's lap. He was startled. He was fifteen years old and it was his first trip to the South. It was politeness on her part. The biscuits were powdery and wonderful. His grandfather said you eat them with gravy. He was telling the boy, whose name was Michael, about the war.

"My war," he said. "The big war. You'll never experience anything like it. I sure as hell hope you don't. You live in a foxhole that's all mud, 'cause it rains for two straight weeks, you sleep in it, you eat in it, then there's thermal pollution."

"What's that?" Michael asked.

His grandfather laughed. "That's when Zumwalt has got you in an ammunition truck that's on fire, the canvas is, and you're driving it out of the compound during a Stuka bombing run and everything is blowing up all around you and the damned truck starts exploding behind you, or you're hunkered down behind a log on the Rhine with the Colonel and a Kraut machine gun is firing from across the water and the slugs are chunking into the log and you can feel them hit and feel the heat from the ones singing off right over your head and both of you crap your pants."

"Were you hit?"

The waitress came over and refilled his grandfather's cup. She poured it really slowly.

"Thank you, Elizabeth," his grandfather said.

The waitress gave Michael's grandfather a smile and shifted her look to Michael and gave him the same smile.

"No." His grandfather laughed again. "But I sure was humiliated."

"Who's Zumwalt?"

"They called him Zip. He was a mean son of a bitch. He'd shoot guys."

"What kind of guys?"

"German ones. Ones that had given up."

The waitress was looking at Michael, watching to see how he was taking it.

"You tell him about your singing, Bub?" the waitress said, holding the coffee pot out. "Maybe something a little more positive?"

"My singing," his grandfather said. "Sit down, Bess," he said to her. She put the glass pot on the table and sat down next to Michael.

His grandfather's name was Bill, but everyone who knew him called him Bub. "When you're with your granddad," Michael's dad had told him, "remember one thing, he's a big talker, so just let him talk. He's got some good stories."

"My singing," his grandfather went on, and it was all about Fridays in Paris, the late spring and summer of 1945 Paris, with all the old architecture, the wonderfully kept parks, the magnificent subway system (wonderfully kept, magnificent,—those were his grandfather's words), and how on leave on those Fridays he would go to this old dance hall with the yellow plaster walls and long, narrow windows up high near the ceiling, the windows always open, to work on his music, and since this would be early afternoon, with the hall not opening until after dark, it was always empty and quiet inside with only the afternoon light coming in, and giving the old woman a five, or sometimes the five and nylon stockings, or a pack of Lucky Strike cigarettes after they talked, and she'd left, giving him the key, he would take the bottle and sit down at the piano, placing the bottle on top.

"Sometimes it was Scotch," he said, "sometimes a nice wine I'd get in this little hole-in-the-wall right up the alley."

And maybe he would sing first, or maybe, after loosening up his hands, he'd play, working on some chords, taking a drink, then start a song, having a drink, singing another song, taking another drink, then a third song, "Laura," "Stars Fell on Alabama," "My Buddy." "Nights are long since you went away, I dream about you all through the day, my buddy, my buddy, your buddy misses you . . ." usually a drink a song, he said, "My Funny Valentine," "Angels with Dirty Faces," "Stardust," going through the lyrics, checking out how they were, how he was, checking the feeling the words and sounds gave him, seeing if the phrasing was working, lighting another Lucky, drifting the phrasing out slowly across the chords, the light inside the hall gradually changing, taking another drink, the light warmer, softer, the pure tingling feeling that came in electric prickles across his forehead and scalp when everything was smoothly working, the alcohol helping, to where he finally would forget where he was and where he'd been, it was only the music, he was not even there, the music was playing him, and he would be sweating and drinking and rocking and smoking and singing and gradually the afternoon would be done, the bottle nearly gone, the cigarettes finished, his voice hoarse, playing just a little longer until time to go, closing the cover over the keys, taking down the bottle, and walking out toward the doors, the light coming through the windows now high on the wall, the long, worn floor nearly dark, going outside, always pleasantly drunk then, locking the doors, putting the key under the stone next to the trash, tossing the bottle into one of the bins, and going on down the alley to Le Cog Vol, The Flying Cock, "That was its real name, Michael," his grandfather said, with inside, the first thing you saw, covering the entire back wall, a ten-foot-high, photographically accurate, wonderful painting of a forty-foot-long, silver-winged erection, the thick swollen pink shaft being straddled by a gorgeous nude, long-legged, full-breasted, with long, flowing chestnut-red hair blowing back off her face in the wind, guiding the cock by means of a black leather bridle strapped just behind the enormous head, her milk-white legs angling back, heels spurring into the pair of gigantic balls, and the little woman who ran this place, hair the brilliant, brittle-looking metallic-red common to most of the women of this quarter, who would say,

"C'etait moi, moi! I was that one. Ah, ah, you should have been here then!"

"And," his grandfather said, "she had a point, kiddo, 'cause you should have seen me back then, at Fort Bliss, back in Texas, when every goddamned guy in the crowd, some six thousand guys, stood and clapped and cheered when I finished singing, McKenzie at the mike calling me back out on the stage, the whistling and cheering still going on, me near to tears, unable to stop shaking. I mean, that was some feeling! Boy, if it wasn't! Of course it was wartime, anyone could've taken that audience, but, hell, at least six thousand guys! And I was slim as an arrow, too!"

"You're still slim, Bub," Bess said.

"Well, that's nice of you to say, Bess," his grandfather said, pushing his mug toward her. "Can't sing like that anymore, though."

"Who was McKenzie, Grandpa?"

"He was the pianist for Sammy Kaye. 'Swing and Sway with Sammy Kaye.' That was one of the biggest orchestras in the country then. Mac heard me singing in the shower during basic training and asked me to sing with them during their USO tour. And so I did."

Bess winked at Michael and got up, topped the cup, then, taking the glass pot, walked off toward another booth to refresh someone else's coffee. Michael waited until she was out of earshot and asked about his grandmother.

His grandfather said, "No, I assumed she'd had other guys. Four years is a long time to be gone. For sure it is when you're young. I never held that against her. I wasn't so perfect myself. Once or twice some strange guy would call on the telephone until they realized I was back. Your dad was just six years old then when I got back, and just as cute as anything could be. I was really glad to see him. And her.

"No, I don't know what happened to Zip. I'm sure he paid for it.

"No different then. No different now.

"All that music is long gone. All Las Vegas lounge act music now, all gone to polyester. Music for lounge lizards."

"I like that music, Bub," Bess said, coming back by again. "It'll always be good music."

She was looking directly at Michael now and he saw that she had soft brown eyes and deep worry lines across her forehead and narrow ones up and down above her upper lip where her skin looked old.

She smiled at him. There was lipstick on the tips of her teeth.

Michael and his grandfather were standing now. His grandfather went over with her to pay the bill. Bess said something that Michael couldn't hear. He saw his grandfather squeeze her hand.

Going outside into the humidity his grandfather said, "Nice little gal, Michael. She's got a good heart."

"She seems to like you, Grandpa. What did she say to you?"

His grandfather laughed.

"Said you were a good-looking boy." He laughed again. "Told her it runs in the family."

Walking up the street to the pickup his grandfather said, "She works hard for her money. She has nice hands. You notice her hands?"

"No," Michael said.

"Very feminine, very fine-boned and gentle, even though she's a working gal."

Michael thought gentle was a strange word to use.

"How do you know her?"

"It's a small town, Michael."

"Do you like her, Grandpa?"

"I certainly do." His grandfather laughed, looking at the boy now. "But not in the way you think."

He put his arm around Michael's shoulders and squeezed them together.

"I'm the one that's gone to polyester," he said.

"What does that mean?"

They were at the pickup now and his grandfather unlocked the doors. Michael could see the fishing rods in their cases were still lying in the bed next to the outboard. He had been worried the whole time that someone was going to take them.

"Well," his grandfather said, "someday I'll explain it to you, but not today. Today's a day for going down to the Keys, and seeing if we can get some of those bull-headed tarps to bite, okay?

"That's the thing about getting out on the water," his grandfather said, getting in, putting the key in the ignition. "Once you get out there all your female troubles just disappear."

He fired up the engine.

"How long will it take us to get there?" Michael asked.

"Just about the time you've digested that breakfast," his grandfather said, turning the wheel, starting them out onto the road.

"What's a bull-headed tarp?"

"Silver tarpon," his grandfather said. "And they're about as nasty as a good-hearted woman when she thinks she's been wronged."

"Sounds like a country-western song," Michael said.

His grandfather laughed.

"That's how they get written," he said.

They rode in silence for a time, going along the coast with the morning clouds still thick and heavy out over the water. Then his grandfather said, "How's your mom?"

"She's good," Michael said.

"She moved back in?"

"She did."

"Good," his grandfather said. "That's good. That's what I wanted to hear. Turn on the radio there, will you? See if you can find some music you like."

Michael smiled at his grandfather. He liked him a lot. Coming down here to go fishing with him had been a good idea.

Mary Anne

"He said there were lots of people I could feel that way with, and I said, 'What good is that? They aren't you.' Which disgusted me, it was such a weak thing to say. I knew I should have slept with someone before I called him, had that security in my head, you know, but I didn't. I called, and ironically, he thought I *had* slept with someone, and so was interested, thinking, I guess, she's not that insecure, and then, after giving in and asking him if he has, and though he doesn't want to tell me, 'God,' he says, 'I have,' then I have to go and tell him I haven't, and my feelings just got out of control, and he just wanted to hang up because it's just too serious and heavy and doesn't feel right at all. So I have no position of interest with him at all, and the only feelings I could move his feelings with were guilt and pity, and I was so close to slipping into them that I started crying right there because I'm so mad at myself, and he says, 'Don't cry,' and I say, 'I'm not crying,' the tears just flooding out of my eyes, 'I'm just upset with myself, is all,' and he says, 'Well, I've got to go,' and I know he does, and he did."

Empty Pockets

The three rides before Jack Cutler bought the bicycle had all been different, but each one came down to the same thing. Each of the drivers wanted sex. The first approach was with photographs.

"I've got some pictures in the glove box you might like," this man said. "Take them out and tell me what you think."

The pictures were in a thick stack in the glove box. Lifting them out, Jack began looking.

First, different naked women standing facing the camera. Then, naked women bending over, their asses to the camera, their legs spread. Next, naked women kissing half-dressed men. Then, naked women and naked men screwing. Then women with women. Then different naked men with erections facing the camera. Then men with men.

Jack Cutler slid them all back together.

The man, a sallow-faced, thirty-five-year-old in a brown suit and a bolo string tie said, "I know it's evil, but I can't help myself. You can't help me, can you? Tell me how I can stop," yet excited looking as he spoke.

Jack put them back in the glove box.

The next man had an old Cadillac without air-conditioning and a real sheriff's badge, which kept him from getting speeding tickets, he said, and a plea, after Jack said, "It's not for me," that he shouldn't think he usually wanted to do this, this was a special circumstance that he knew he would pay for later, that just to have these thoughts was a sin.

The feeling off this man was slightly different than off the previous man. This man was genuinely upset. It was as hot inside the car as it was outside, and Jack thought, How can people stand this heat? His T-shirt was soaked in sweat.

The third ride was into Pensacola, this driver saying his

mother was dying of cancer and he was only driving up and down the highway as he didn't know what else to do. She was hospitalized right now, and he would drive Jack as far as Mobile, he had nothing better to do, if Jack would. Then he got mad and said, "I could kill you. I could strangle you in your own spit, you know that?" They were already into the industrial section on the outskirts of Pensacola.

Jack looked at the gray stubble under the dyed-black mustache, the broken vein in the man's right eye. The man's hair was coal black and shiny like it had been painted. Jack didn't know what to say, so he said, "You think your mother would like that?"

"You're getting your scrawny ass out here," the man said, then softened his voice and warned Jack to watch out for the niggers, that he was likely to get his head broke if he tried sleeping off the road and wasn't careful, that every year some unknown white boy was found dead along these roads, usually a northern white boy, dead with a fractured skull, that this country had no place for people who didn't belong here. "You hear what I'm sayin' to you?"

"Sure," Jack said, getting out. "Thanks. I'll remember that."

It was a long walk into the heat-drenched town carrying the duffel. Jack bought some grilled chicken on a stick from some kind of a Cuban street vendor and then saw a pawnshop and went inside.

There was a big silver floor fan set up on the glass counter blowing warm air toward the doorway. The air was really warm. It took a moment for Jack's eyes to adjust. He tried on a pair of snakeskin cowboy boots that fit him like they had been custom made. They were six dollars. He thought very carefully about them. He only had thirteen dollars left. What was six dollars? In L.A. they would cost two hundred. If he could find them. How far would seven dollars take him? How far would thirteen? The bicycle was five dollars. Jack was sick of homos and rides from homos. The bike was an old-fashioned American standard, large balloon tires, single-speed sprocket, a black rubber pedal on the left, only a shiny steel peg on the right. The pawnbroker didn't have another pedal.

"It's still a good deal," he said, over his toothpick.

It was dusk by the time Jack made his way through Pensacola.

He knew he couldn't sleep under the city pier, not knowing what the tides were doing, but it felt good to be moving in the humid air on the old road to Mobile. He pedaled easily for some time, the canvas duffel strapped across the thick handlebars, glad he'd spent the money for the bike, with all the landscape lying quietly and clearly in front of him, detailing exactly how everything was so he didn't miss any of it.

He was well out of the city by now, and he rode across a concrete bridge raised some thirty feet over a wide, lush delta and a shallow, meandering river. He stopped and got off and stood there for a while. The evening star was out and the sky was rose colored and reflected off the surface of the water. Swallows were flying out from under the arches of the bridge, working in long, then quick, turning curves and slashes in the darkening air above the river grasses.

Jack wondered what they were feeding on.

His legs felt good and he felt good, but about ten miles farther out a truck came by and almost hit him, honking its horn as it swerved out of the way, and he began to worry about riding in the dark.

It was almost an hour later when he came into Magnolia Springs.

Across the road was a hardware store with its lights on. The building was old and painted yellow. He rode across and rested the bike against the wall. There was a veranda, and a bell jangled as he crossed the threshold.

From the backroom a woman's voice called, "Be right there." A short, gray-haired woman with her hair tied back in a bun, wiping her hands on an apron, came out.

"I was pouring out some old coffee," she said. "What can I do for you?"

He told her, and she left and brought back a box of reflectors. He took a big, round red one and asked if she had some scrap wire. The reflector was sixty-five cents, and she brought the wire when he was outside trying to figure out where to tie it on.

"Why don't y'all tie it under the seat?" She sat down on the steps. "Hang it from the coils."

"That's a good idea," Jack said, already starting to wire it into place.

"Where y'all coming from?"

"Pensacola."

"Lord, that's a long way. You mean you rode that bicycle from Pensacola?"

"Yes, ma'am," he said. "It's not that far."

"Let me fix us some coffee," she said.

Jack sat down on the steps. She came out with the coffee and sat down again. Across the road the streetlight was swarming with bugs. Her oldest boy was dead in Vietnam, she said, he'd been about Jack's age.

"His name was William, but we always called him Beau. Were you in the war?"

"No," Jack said, "I got out of it."

"I'm glad," she said. "Let me get you some more coffee."

"No, I don't want to bother you. I should get going."

"It's no bother," she said.

"No, I need to go."

"Where are you going to sleep?"

"Somewhere down the road," Jack said.

She reached out her hand and touched his, held on to it for a moment, and he thanked her again, giving her the coffee cup, and walked off the porch and got on the bike and waved good-bye to her.

For the next few blocks a dog began chasing and barking at him and then fell back. It was quiet for a while, and then he was moving up alongside a wide waterway with the road running empty of cars. Lights came from houseboats moored on the far shore. Voices sounded across the water, and he saw the silhouettes of a man and woman standing inside a lit doorway of a houseboat facing each other, the air smelling of brine and oil and mud. And then it was dark and he pedaled until much later, swarms of mosquitoes attacking him as he rode, and slept on the floor of a tiny laundromat on the outskirts of Mobile that luckily had screens on the windows. Some of the mosquitoes had been biting right through his jeans. He never knew they could do that. He'd always hated mosquitoes, and now he hated them even more.

He was really glad to be off the road.

"It's the cold," the pawnbroker had said. "I think the cold keeps it repressed and they get down here in the heat and just let go.

"They drive down from Chicago, all them northern boys. What they do is rent an entire motel, like the Windjammer down in the Keys, that's got all the rooms facing an inner corridor, 'n' once everybody's checked in, unlock all the inside doors to every room, 'n' then go around and lock all the outside doors so's no one else can get in.

"About a hundred of them boys all through the holidays, never go outside once. Not even to eat, bring all their own food with 'em, see.

"Them are the boys that musta been picking you up."

In the morning Jack's body was stiff, his thighs swollen, and his right foot sore from the steel peg. There were bites all over his body, and blood on his lower back and the side of his neck that came off in smears on his fingers.

When he went out the air was already muggy and, following the road inland along a bayou, a warm wind rippling the brown water, Jack went by a series of fishing shacks on posts in the low tide mud, then along the tree-shaded road past a mile of abandoned-looking, tin-sided warehouses, and on out into the real countryside with the wind dying as the heat increased.

Everything was pedaling, pedaling, pedaling.

Purple and red flowers wildly lined the road. A farmhouse cleanly white in the distance was surrounded in thick waves of elms. The bicycling grew harder, and he was standing, counting the strokes, going up another hill, then he was coasting, the wind blowing the heat off his face. Far ahead the road had water on it. The tires ran silently. There were fields and fields and fields.

The trees were spread far apart, stilled, growing, looming up. The spokes caught the wind and howled. Birds curved leftward above the trees. The road leveled off. The heat was pulling sweat from him in warm rivulets. His T-shirt was soaked. Everything was dreamlike. He needed something to eat. He let the bike coast on out and fade to a halt. He got off and walked. The trees were in closer, growing right to the edges of the road. You could only see a little way in between them. He pushed the bike, ate an orange, and got back on again and started slowly moving his legs, not trying to do anything but quietly ride.

He rode all morning, drinking water as he went, rarely seeing any cars, the landscape heavily wooded now, more pine than deciduous, desolate, the heat seeming to change in density with each mile he went. The arch of his right foot was beginning to ache, and he thought, I should get some pieces of wood and tie them together on the peg.

His foot really began to hurt and, coming to an abandoned watermelon stand, he stopped to rest and find some wood to tie onto the peg.

He rested the bike against a corner of the stand and looked around; maybe there would be a well with some water to refill his bottle. All around him the landscape was perfectly quiet.

There was nothing and going inside he lay down on a bench under the broken roof and looked up at the sky. Towering cathedrals of clouds, sun-filled in their centers, drifted across the broken opening. The air was so hot it was palpable.

The pawnbroker said the woods were full of snakes, that snakes would be on the move looking for water because of the heat.

Jack leaned over and looked under the bench.

"If you smell cucumbers," he'd said, "that's a copperhead. My momma got bit by one. She was picking peaches and jumped down by a fence and got bit on her ankle. Every year at the same time her ankle'll turn the color of copper, with purple patches on it. You don't wanna go off the road and camp in the woods. Hope is your best shot with a cottonmouth. There ain't nothin' else you can do. Just make sure you don't step nowhere near one."

Outside the road glistened, the surface of the asphalt a slick black as the heat brought up the tar. The tires of the bike were heavy with the tar.

How much hotter could it get?

Wiping sweat off his face, he lay back down, grateful for the shade.

Another enormous cloud drifted across the edge of the roofing.

When Jack awoke he realized he hadn't even known he'd fallen asleep and, sitting up, saw that his thighs were even more swollen. He had to walk around for several minutes to get them loose enough to get on the bicycle again. He had cooled down some, but the air seemed even heavier than when he fell asleep, and within three minutes of riding he was again drenched in sweat.

He hadn't fixed the pedal and every time he pushed, pain shot through the arch. He pedaled on his toes, but after a while that began to hurt. On the flats he would pedal mostly one legged. When he came to the slightest grade he got off and walked, pushing the bike.

The sky was completely clouded over now, and coming down a long hill he saw a small crossroads store painted dark brown. Two yellow gas pumps stood on concrete biscuits in the dirt driveway. The roof was tin that extended out as a canopy for the pumps.

As Jack bumped off the pavement and rolled onto the dirt he saw a large Jax Beer, a large Nehi, and a smaller red Coca-Cola sign nailed along the open door and a long wood bench against the wall. He was really thirsty. He got off the bike and walked it over to the store, then leaned it up against the wall. There was an outhouse against the stand of pines behind the store, and at the side of the steps a thin black hose coming out from a spigot.

He ran the water for a moment and started to drink. The water was warm and had a rubbery, bitter taste, and he spat it out and then ran the water over his head and neck, letting it soak into his T-shirt.

He could hear voices coming from inside the store and he turned the water off, coiled the hose, and set it back down on the dirt.

The store was dark inside and the floor creaked as he walked in and the voices stopped.

An old man was sitting on a stool behind the counter and two other men were sitting in chairs by the ice cooler. Jack walked over to the cooler, slid open the door and reached down in the cold water and fished out a glass bottle of Coke. He popped the cap in the bottle opener, then picked out four yellow apples from a peach basket full and carried them to the counter.

"That's a dollar 'n' two bits," the old man said, "less'n you're not drinking the Coke here."

"No, I'll drink it here," Jack said. "I'll drink it out on the bench."

The old man didn't have any teeth in his mouth. They were in a water glass by the cash register. An open tin of Copenhagen was next to the glass. He obviously chewed the tobacco without his teeth. There was a small, barefoot boy with close-cropped blond hair and blue coveralls standing next to one of the men in the chairs, staring at Jack.

"Y'all's a Yankee," the old man said as Jack put the apples on the counter.

"No, sir," Jack said.

"Yes'n you are."

"Y'all ain't stirrin' up trouble, are ya?" came a voice from the corner.

This was the skinny little man in the farmer coveralls whose eyes Jack had felt on him when he took out the Coke.

"What trouble?"

"Niggra trouble," the little man said.

"No, sir," Jack said.

"Tha's good," the old man said. "Tha's good. Where y'all from?"

"California," Jack answered.

"California," said the little man, looking over at the old man behind the counter. "A Californian is the one that's shot Medgar Evers."

He looked at Jack. "You know that?"

"Who's Medgar Evers?"

The old man behind the counter laughed. "One of them uppity niggras that lived in Jackson."

"California's fulla queers," the little man said, "you know that?"

"I don't know that," Jack said.

"You go to school?" Jack said to the boy.

"I ain't big enough," the boy said.

"How old are you?"

"Six."

"Lemme explain it to you," the storekeeper said. "People like you don't know the history of the South. After the war them niggras, or colored folk, whatever you want to call 'em, was as bad as could be. Hell, they was rapin' 'n' lootin' 'n' killin', getting all big headed, causing the worst of their own troubles. Now that's how the Ku Klux Klan rose up. Keep 'em from taking everything, see."

Jack glanced over at the little boy, who was staring back at him. The other man, sitting back in the shadows, said, "Why you lookin' at my boy?"

"I'm not," Jack said.

He took out five quarters and laid them on the counter, pushing them to the old man.

"You know why niggras have big nostrils?" the little man said.

Jack didn't answer.

"'Cause they got big fingers," he said, laughing.

Jack took the apples and the Coke, glanced back at the two men and the little boy, and walked outside.

Far off across the road, rain was slashing down into a hillside of trees. The rain was blue gray with sunlight at the edges. He sat down on the bench and watched it lashing the trees in marching columns of shifting smoke, leaving everything behind a bright, gleaming green. He put the apples on the bench. The Coke bottle was cold from being in the icy water of the metal cooler and he pressed it against his temples and cheeks, then the sides of his neck, before drinking it.

He could hear the same voices coming from inside, but he wasn't listening to what they were saying. He didn't care what they were saying. He took the Coke down in several long, smooth swallows, feeling the burn in his nostrils and throat.

There was an open wood box by the doorway half-filled with empty pop bottles and he got up and put the bottle in one of the slots, then walked back and picked up the apples, taking them with him out into the heat, tucking them inside the duffel, and got on the bike, thinking how quickly the sky had clouded over.

He rode out onto the roadway, going up a slight hill along a split-log pine fence. Far up the hillside a band of horses stood side by side, not moving, nose to tail, tail to nose, heads drooped to the ground, not feeding, the heat too heavy for their bones.

As Jack came closer, the air extremely heavy now, he expected them to move or to look up, but they did neither, just stayed as they were. And suddenly the rain broke, silver sheets drenching everything, Jack could barely see, soaking everything through and through, everything immediately cool, three days and nights of steadily numbing heat gone in an instant, all the horses suddenly whirling, two sprinting off in the sheer joy of the rain, the bay revealing itself as a thoroughbred racing full out, rapidly away down the fence line, a brown blur washing out in the silver.

And just as suddenly the rain was gone, and Jack rode until dusk, sometimes walking, sometimes coasting, seeing nothing save the second-growth pine mixed with the deciduous trees and the thick tangles of brush. The pine was patched with blister rust, and once Jack thought he saw a snake vanishing into a dry clump of grasses and he didn't like the feeling it gave him.

That night he slept in an empty farmhouse on top of a broken kitchen table, hanging the duffel up on a nail so nothing could crawl into it, then taking his jeans off and folding them into a pillow. For a time he sat up in the dark, eating an apple, stretching his legs out, trying to get comfortable.

Jack lay down on his side. He was really, really tired. His foot really ached.

He wondered who it was that had lived in this house. The woods were thick right at the doorstep. It wasn't what was called a shotgun shack, one room with two doors, the front and back, so small that you could shoot a shotgun straight through it and not hit anything inside. There was still a faint dusty smell of kerosene, or was it coal oil? It had three rooms, the kitchen, the larger room, and a small room that must have been where they all slept. Since it had a kitchen, probably there were women and children who lived here as well as men.

A night bird called from somewhere, and then another and, closing his eyes, there weren't any mosquitoes, and in the morning when Jack woke he saw he hadn't turned at all. He was still on his left side, his legs bent under him, but they were so cramped he had to pound his thighs with his fists before he could straighten them out. Then he found he couldn't get his jeans on.

He took his pocketknife out and cut slits along the inseams, then slid his legs in.

He put his boots on and ate an apple and studied the map, seeing the road would take him almost into Meridian before veering off past the big highway into Jackson. He measured the distance he had come, it was already over a hundred miles, and then drank the last of his water and went outside with the bicycle and the duffel, finding a piece of shingle on the ground.

He broke it with his hands and went back inside, looking for a coat hanger or a bit of wire.

There wasn't anything in the front room, and as he walked back into the kitchen he saw a gray-and-black rattlesnake silently moving along the base of the kicked-in cabinets under the sink. It wasn't big, maybe a foot and a half in length, but thick and ugly.

Jack watched it for a moment.

It was going up into the cabinets.

He turned and went back outside. It wasn't rational, but he didn't want to fix the pedal now and, strapping the duffel onto the handlebars, he took the bike and pushed on out toward the road, going down the dirt track, watching carefully ahead into the grass at the side of the ruts. There hadn't been any water in back in the well. The rusted pump handle hadn't worked. He'd dropped a rock inside the well, but only a stone sound came back. The snake was only trying to do what he had to do: get more water.

This idea of bicycling the back roads to Arkansas was really dumb. If it were cooler, it wouldn't be. Well, it wasn't cooler. He'd wanted to see the South. He was seeing it, all right, going about it as stupidly as he possibly could.

Calm down, he told himself. Just calm down.

Back on the bike, the air still warm, the sky everywhere a soft blue, his legs warming up, he felt a lot better, his foot not hurting that much. He took out an apple and began to eat it, but within a few miles heat lines began to rise off the asphalt, hovering in the distance, and the sky began turning white.

It was already hill country now, and he began walking the bike up each hill, then getting on and coasting the down slopes, the front wheel of the bike going into a wobble that threatened to wreck the bearings, not seeing anything, just feeling the heat and his own sweat, hearing the tires making the swishing sound.

He knew if he stopped his legs would cramp, but he had one apple left and he could eat it and for a while he'd be okay.

If the bicycle itself lasted.

Well, let it wreck itself, he thought. To keep on with the bicycle would be even dumber. He knew he couldn't take much more. He'd go until he heard a car coming, then he was going to quit and start hitchhiking again. He didn't care who was coming down the road.

Then he heard a car coming and pulled over and got off and waited. He couldn't see anything at first then saw a black car coming down around the curve of trees.

As it approached it slowed and went past, and then slowed again and began to stop, the taillights coming on, pulling over just below the next hill, dust coming up and powdering the car as it finally stopped and sat there, the engine pinging.

Heat lines shimmied off the hood.

Jack waited, holding on to the bike.

Behind the heat lines a large man in a white shirt and black slacks got out and stood by the door and called something out.

The man was hatless, and Jack called back, "Can't hear you."

He started wheeling the bike down toward the man. Half-shielded by the car door, there was something wrong about the man as he stood there waiting.

"What did you say?" Jack called, closer to the car now, the engine still making that pinging sound.

"Don't make me say it again," the man said, moving out from behind the car door.

"Say what again?"

"Ten bucks, boy."

"Ten bucks?" Jack said, pushing the bike closer, seeing the man clearly now, a large man with gray hair combed sideways over a sweaty head, one brown eye that cast inward toward the nose, a silver crucifix dangling on a chain around a sweaty, double-chinned neck.

"Is that what you said? I thought you said something else."

The man hesitated, "I said . . . I said I want to suck your cock."

"You want to suck my cock?"

"Twenty dollars. I'll give you twenty dollars."

"Sure," Jack said, dropping the bike, doubling up his fists, moving fast toward the car. "You can suck it after I bust your goddamn, cross-eyed face!"

The man's eyes blinked and his face twisted and he turned and bolted, hurrying himself to get back in the car, hitting into the door, the door not closing, grinding the starter after the engine caught, crashing the gears, the door closing, a stream of dirty blue smoke spreading from under the bumper as the car u-turned and sped off back the way it came.

Jack watched it go.

Cicadas were whirring from everywhere in the woods.

It was weird that he hadn't noticed them before.

Jesus Christ, Jack thought, it's so goddamn hot. This fucking heat is going to kill me.

Walking back to the bike, he picked it up.

The droning mixed with the heat was starting to make him feel sick.

Slowly, he got back on the bike, starting to pedal up the long, gradual slope of the hill, every several seconds thinking, How much farther can I go, and, halfway up, had to get off and walk, unable to pump any longer.

He took out the apple, eating all of it, sucking on the seeds to keep moisture in his mouth, thinking I'll sit and rest, but there was no shade anywhere save off in the tangled thickets under the thousands of motionless trees.

Cicadas were whirring from everywhere.

No way was he going in there.

No other cars passed him at all, either coming or going.

All that existed was heat, the road, the thousands of trees, the thickets, the cicadas, the seeds in his mouth gone dry. He spat them out and just walked in the layers of heat, his body drenched in sweat.

He would need water soon.

He reached the top of the slope and got back on the bike and began coasting downhill, not braking, letting the bike go, the front wheel starting into its wobble, threatening to fly off as he hit the flat where he began furiously pedaling again to reach as much speed as he could to gain height onto this next hill coming up before getting off and walking again.

Funny how it was water you wanted. Nothing else.

He attacked three hills before he quit.

Going down this last long dry grade in the now crackling heat, the trees rushing by, he knew his legs were finished. There was no way he could turn around. He'd gone too far to go back. He'd just push the bike off to the side and just keep walking, but then it was easier to let the bike carry the duffel. What did he need the duffel for anyway? What was it carrying? Two T-shirts, a jacket, some socks, underwear, the map, the empty water bottle, some raisins?

The raisins. He'd forgotten about the raisins.

Jack stopped and took the duffel off, unclipping the snap from the brass eyelet, the metal singeing his fingers. He found the raisins and unwrapped them, the raisins half-melted together.

He heard another car coming and, looking up, saw a narrow red clay road going up into the woods and then a black-and-orange pickup truck appearing through some trees and then vanishing again, the engine growing louder all the time.

After a moment it came out along the road and turned onto the highway.

He stuck his thumb out.

It went by, dusty-looking, three white men inside.

He ate the raisins and picked up the bike again, strapping the duffel back on.

Jack walked along, wheeling the bike.

Around the curve was another hill.

Okay, he thought, this is it, the very last one. I'll do it. Walk up, coast the slope, then dump the bike. No one will pick me up if I have the bike.

Goddamn, Jack thought, I'm goddamn burning to death!

There were millions of cicadas sawing away as he walked. He didn't remember hearing them before. Of course he'd heard them before, heard that one long constant, unrelenting, endless drone. It was the heat. The goddamn heat was screwing up his head. His skin was burning. Now that he was listening he thought there were so many of them that the trees would begin lifting off the ground. He wiped his face. What was that thought? That their wings would lift up the trees?

Whose thoughts are these? he thought. Are these even your own thoughts? These aren't even your own thoughts. Just dump the bike.

Why don't you?

Jack kept moving, sweat dripping off his face, pacing slowly along the trees, not looking at anything.

Just before the crest of the hill, where the trees came in over the road, he saw another diamondback, this one run over just before it had reached the centerline, dead, crushed just behind the head, blood puddled out on the asphalt.

He stopped and looked, the unrelenting droning of the cicadas going on.

The rattler was over four feet long, thick as a forearm, all gray and black, deadly looking, bits of mangled pinkish flesh sticking out from under the thin layer of yellowish top skin over the pattern of diamonds.

That pickup must have got him. That orange-and-black pickup. He's on this side of the road. He must have just come out of the woods. Two bottle flies were walking in the blood by the head, their bodies iridescent green. The snake's eyes were brightly dark under the hood. The blood was still wet.

Jack was afraid to touch him.

The ride you didn't get, he thought.

What makes you think it's a him?

Good Christ, he thought, listen to yourself.

You need water, he thought. You really, really need water.

Jack turned and began pushing the bike again. It hurt now to step on his right foot. His mouth was chalky, his tongue fat and stuck against the roof of his mouth. He never should have kept those seeds. Maybe it was the raisins. He really wanted to drink. He'd drink anything that was wet. It didn't have to be water.

Listen to that, he thought. You've got to get some water.

He reached the crest and got on the bicycle, looking far down the slope, seeing that even in this heat how beautiful the woods looked, the dark road curving out of view around the trees on the right, and then he pushed off only to find he couldn't put any kind of pressure on his foot.

He began pedaling with his left leg only, holding his right leg out free from the turning crank.

The slope was gradual in descent, and he slowly picked up speed, and though hot, there was wind, the flow of it over his face and neck a relief, the speed picking up, and then down and around the long curve he went, almost leaning over, the road plunging now into a long straight toward the floor of what was a little valley with the front wheel gone into its furious wobble and the treed landscape rushing by, and suddenly he felt good and thought, Hell, one more hill. I can do that. I'll do just one more.

The flat was like the bottom curve of a large round bowl and, though the woods ran close on the left, on the right lay a long yellowing field of waist-high weeds and grasses that ran half a hundred yards back to a small, empty-looking, bare boarded house with a shaded front porch up on blocks set back against a hillside heavy with trees.

Two small black children came running out from the house and, just as Jack reached the flat, began racing through the tall weeds toward the road. They were waving their arms, yelling as they came, two little whips of a black boy and girl, their shirts a royal blue, their shouts lost in the wind.

Going as fast as he'd ever gone, the front wheel shaking, taking him almost out of control, flying past the kids, Jack began pedaling again, not feeling any pain at all, pushing himself even harder. Let's see how far you can go, he thought. You can go farther, maybe you're not done at all.

Going past the end of the field, heading up the grade, the bike already slowing, the front wheel no longer wobbling, Jack continued hard, gaining more distance, then his left leg seized up, a knifing pain burning down his thigh right through the knee and into his foot. He tried to pedal once more, and again the pain seared through him, and he totally and completely quit. He just couldn't do it. That was it. He was completely done. It was over.

The bike slowed, Jack letting it, and then slowly stopped, the droning of the cicadas just maniacal, sweat pouring off him.

Looking back around, he saw the children standing halfway up the slope to the road, silently looking at him.

Okay, he thought, and slowly got off, and turned with the bike and walked back toward them, thinking maybe they have some water in the house. If I can get some water and take a rest I can go on with the bike.

The children were motionless as Jack approached, the boy standing in the weeds slightly in front of the girl, both thin as string, skin so pure a black that in the direct sunlight it had a gunmetal, bluish sheen, with close-cropped heads that seemed too large for their bodies.

"Hello," Jack said.

They didn't answer, their large dark eyes completely watching him.

"Do you know where I can get a drink of water?"

Suddenly the boy dipped his head, turned, and then both of them began running flat out through the tall grasses back toward the house.

Jack watched them go, both moving fast across the field.

Just a stride ahead of the girl, the boy reached the house and was up the steps and inside, the little girl following.

The dirt track from the road up to the house looked as if only people walking had made it. Jack didn't know what to do. The narrow porch fronting the house was dark and empty.

He stood still, holding on to the bike.

Save for the cicadas, everything was silent. Then a woman came out onto the porch. She was a very big black woman, as big as a big man, in a brilliant maroon housedress, a red bandanna capping her head. She stopped at the top of the steps and stared out at Jack. Then the little boy stepped out, his arm raised and pointing, excitedly talking, looking back into the shadowed doorway.

Then more women came out: one, two, three, four of them, each nearly as large as the big woman, each deeply black, each wearing a different colored bandanna tied about her head, each in a differently colored floral-print dress: turquoise, purple, green, yellow . . .

Then the big woman waved, motioning Jack to come to them, all the women staring out at him.

Jack got back on the bike and pushed off, coasting back down the road to the dirt track, then turned in and bumped down the slope and let go, letting the bike fall into the weeds, unstrapping the duffel from the handlebars.

He counted five women as he walked with the duffel toward the house, along with the little boy and now the little girl appearing again. Then three other women came out on the porch: the first two small and thin, the third one tall and light-skinned, each dressed in bright floral-print housedresses, each in a head scarf of a brilliant blue or red or black, all eight of them standing there with the children, watching as he approached up the path.

The big woman wore tennis shoes; all the others were barefoot. The thinnest one had her hands on the little girl's shoulders, an older woman. The big woman had the boy, holding his narrow arm by the bicep, the boy gone silent now, his eyes wide as he watched Jack.

Jack reached the steps and stopped, tiny dark spots floating across his eyes.

He and the big woman looked at each other for a moment. She had a strong, broad face with smooth, rounded-looking cheekbones, a wide, flat nose, and almost black, impossible to read eyes.

Jack suddenly felt dizzy.

"Hello," she said.

"Hello," Jack answered, glancing at the boy, then back at her. "Could I trouble you for a drink of water?

"I'm very thirsty."

"Of course, child," the big woman said. "C'mon up here," and she turned to the woman that held the little girl and said, "Momma."

This woman turned and went inside the doorway.

"May the children look at your bicycle?"

The boy's eyes were moving on Jack's eyes, the big woman still holding him close.

"Sure," Jack said, wiping his face, trying to clear his vision. "They can have it."

The little boy's eyes went wider, his face turning to the big woman for confirmation.

"'They can have it?'"

"It's yours," he said to the boy. "Yours and your sister's."

"Oh, hallelujah!" the big woman said, letting the boy go, and down the steps he flew, his sister right behind him, racing out past Jack, the little girl yelling, "Me first. Me first!"

"Oh, praise Jesus!" the big woman said, "Oh, thank you, Jesus!

"You mean it?" she said, looking down at Jack.

"Absolutely," Jack said. "I'm finished. I can't pedal it any farther."

"Oh, Jesus be praised!" she said, and suddenly all the other women began echoing her. "Oh, Jesus be praised! Oh, Jesus be praised!" Each saying over and over, "Oh, thank you, Jesus! Oh, Jesus be praised! Oh, dear sweet Jesus! Oh, thank you, Jesus . . ."

"Now y'all comes on up here 'n' gets out of the sun," the big woman said, all the women now smiling at him, their voices all crossing in a chorus, all saying, "Oh, yes, oh, my yes, oh, thank you, Jesus, oh, thank you, dear sweet Jesus, oh, thank you, oh, thank you, Jesus," and as Jack started up the steps somehow a chair was produced, and the big woman was telling him she would invite him in, but there was only one room, and Gram'momma was down sick, and she was sorry, "Oh, praise Jesus," her face very happy, all the other women continuing, "Oh, thank you, Lord, oh, praise be to Jesus," then the woman called Momma came out with a large blue glass, handing it to Jack, the glass very cold to the touch, of a fluted, translucent, deep aqua blue, as large as a milkshake container, holding, as he lifted it to his mouth and drank, the coldest, cleanest, most pure water he had ever tasted.

He couldn't believe it.

Dropping the duffel, Jack drank and drank and drank, all the women continuing to thank Jesus, telling him they all had been praying since before last Christmas for a bicycle for the children and had been telling them to trust that Jesus would not disappoint them and when they saw him coming down the hill they knew he was coming with their bicycle.

"No way coulds I keep 'em back from runnin' out to meets you," the big woman said.

The water was absolute bliss.

They got him another glassful, and a third, and a cold washrag, and Jack cooled his face and the back of his neck, and the whole time the women kept saying, "Oh, praise, Jesus," and finally, cooled down, he got up, handing the beautiful blue glass back to the big woman, thanked them all, nodding to the older woman called Momma, looked into the house, a hot, musty smell coming from inside the small, dark room, then turned, taking up his duffel, and stiffly walked back down the steps out into the strength-sapping heat and sunlight, and out onto the dusty track going by the little girl up on the seat of the bicycle being pushed by the boy, both very happy, and on past the yellowing grasses and finally up onto the heated road where almost before he had time to turn and wave to the women, all standing on the porch watching, he was picked up by a middle-aged white guy with a truck driver's belly and red sideburns with a yellow, plastic snap-tabbed baseball hat driving a blue-and-white Colonial Bread step van who, when they were passed by two blacks in an old Chevrolet a few miles farther on, floored the van and raced after them flat out at fifty-five miles an hour, the van actually shuddering the whole time, not even for a second coming within sight of the Chevy, the speedometer needle quivering right around the fifty-five mark, completely pissed off that two blacks had had the nerve to pass him, saying, "That's what that fuckin' cocksucker John Kennedy 'n' his brother Bobby did to this country. Lettin' all them niggras think they can run everybody, them cocksuckers are takin' over everything!"

Morrison, he said his name was, racing the van like that all the way into Meridian, spilling most of the bread off the side shelves in the process, in between offering Jack drinks of J.T.S. Brown from a glass bottle.

"The best bourbon," he said, "in the whole entire goddamn United States of America."

Rawlins

I t was blowing again when Davis walked back, the wind coming hard down the cut along the switching tracks, the parked rows of empty boxcars hot sided and dead looking against the hillside of fine blowing dust sheeting behind them. A haze of dust was drifting east down the roofs of the cars, and coming back to the motel there were fire engines in the alley, the burned tool shed still smoldering, with the smoke mixing in the dust and the wino off one of the freights, who had apparently gone in, started a fire, and fallen asleep, being carried out badly burned and not expected to live.

In the room Kathy and Glen were no longer playing Monopoly and the sequence of pills had worked, Joni was finished, and the doctor was coming out of the little bathroom with the steel pan full of the yellowish clear fluid mixed with blood standing there showing them the fetus. It was tiny, curled, and pinkish like a shrimp, and the fluid stank, and Kathy wouldn't look at it, but Joni did and didn't say anything, then said, "That's my baby," and said it again, disgusting Glen who went outside with the doctor to give him the other five hundred.

Glen's little brother was the one who had gotten Joni pregnant, with Glen getting him out of it, and Joni was crying now and was still crying when Glen came back in. He told her to knock it off, to not confuse, "What could be with what is."

Then they started another game of Monopoly without Joni.

She had a fever and Kathy kept leaving the game to go ice her down. Finally Glen won the game, having two hotels each on Park Place and on Boardwalk, which broke everyone.

In the morning Joni was better and ready to leave. The wind had stopped blowing and the sky was clear, but there was dust all over everything, and in the car going back to Boulder she told Glen she was in love with him. She made a big deal about it. She was sincere about it. She was riding up front with Glen. Kathy and Davis sat in the back. Davis was looking out at the desert. Kathy said to Joni, "Please, shut up."

A New Pair of Shoes

SHERIFF'S DEPUTY R. O. HERNANDEZ:

"The subject was facedown, the soles of his shoes facing the ceiling of the car. He didn't respond or react to my tapping on the window. Using a wire I fished open the lock latch. There was no movement from him the entire time. Upon entry I pulled at his legs. They were stiff. There was no pulse. The hands were cold, with the fingers stiff. A coat of a brown rayon-like material was draped over the head. No ID was found on his person."

MR. ROBERT GAINES:

"He came to the door right at closing time, him, and the gentleman over there. He said no one was going to push him around, he was coming in to see his brother. I let them in and they went by me. Then there was a banging-like in the office, then all of a sudden this strange screaming but choking-like sound, like someone couldn't get their breath—that was Bill, I guess—then they came wrestling out, Vic with his hands squeezing around Bill's neck, both of them rolling around. We jumped in there like a shot, trying to get Vic off him. It took both of us to pry them loose. Bill was trying to talk, you know, crying-like, 'cause he'd been choked, just lying there, but still trying to fight.

"Finally he stopped fighting.

"Both Mr. McNulty there and I had Victor over in the corner and we let Bill up and then this white stuff started coming out his mouth and he put his arms up above his head, and all of a sudden he starts this growling way down deep in his throat-like, and before we knew it he's going after Vic again.

"Well, I tripped him and then Vic jumps in, slugging him on the back, yelling, 'Bill, Bill, I'm your brother, your brother!' you know, trying to calm him down, then Mr. McNulty grabbed Victor and pulled him off.

"Bill wasn't moving. He was lying facedown. There wasn't anything coming out of his mouth now. It was shut, and so were his eyes. 'He's out of it,' Mr. McNulty kept saying.

"I said, 'I hope to Christ you didn't hit him too hard, Vic.'

"Vic was saying, 'He's my brother, he's my goddamn brother!'

"To me, neither of them, McNulty or Vic, were making much sense, but McNulty was trying to help. He had the front of Bill's body, trying to pull it out from Vic, but Vic had Bill's arm twisted behind his back, crying and yelling at him things like, 'I'm your brother,' which I already said, and that if he didn't listen to him and calm down he was gonna get his arm broke.

"He, Bill, wasn't moving, though. Vic had hit him on the back when he'd fallen down.

"Hard, I'd say, fairly hard. And he, Bill, Mr. Galen that is, went still, kind of sagging-like.

"There was no way of knowing whether he was conscious or not.

"I finally told McNulty to let it go. And then Vic let go, too.

"I don't know whose idea it was, but we picked Bill up and took him out to the car. I guess it was Vic's idea.

"Anyway, he, Bill, was motionless all the way out to the car. I asked Vic if he thought Bill would be all right. He said, 'Yeah, he's done this before. We'll just let him sleep it off.'

"Thinking about it now, I remember he moved around for a few minutes there after he was hit.

"No, sir, we didn't think he was hurt that bad, I guess."

AUTOPSY REPORT:

"Scrapes and bruises on the cheeks and bruises on the forehead. Small hemorrhages on the skin indicating the body had been lying facedown for some time. The blood had settled. An extreme amount of congestion in the lungs: approximately 745 to 800 grams. A normal amount for a man of this size and age is 250 to 300 grams. Death resulted from pulmonary congestion and edema; that is, he suffocated to death."

"Yes, sir, I believe at least three or four drinks. Vodka doubles, with a side of orange juice and a side of water, all in separate glasses.

"Yes, I believe he was drunk at the time.

"When we left the Wagon Wheel he asked would I like a pair of shoes. I said, 'Sure.'

"We drove out to his brother's store and had a hassle about getting in, then went in the back into the office.

"Billy, Mr. Galen that is, told Mr. Galen there, Victor, to fix his buddy up—that was me—with a pair of shoes, good dress shoes.

"Mr. Galen there said something like, 'No, not now. We're too busy.'

"He was sitting at his desk and had his computer on, and he turned around in his chair with his back to us, one of those swivel office chairs, and all of a sudden Billy lunged for him and grabbed him around the neck.

"No, sir, I'd never met Mr. Galen before. That was our first meeting. I knew Billy several months before that. We were working at the Salvation Army and were on Disulfiram or Antabuse, as it's commonly called, and got enough money collected to go out and get one tied on.

"No, sir, I didn't know the car was stolen. I thought it was Mr. Galen's, Bill Galen's, that is.

"No, sir, we didn't put no coat over his head, though we tried. That is, I don't think there was no coat over his head. I don't remember whether there was or not. I think I tried to pull that coat up over his head, but when I started to I got scared and felt foolish and—

"No, sir, I didn't know if he was dead or not."

MR. VICTOR GALEN:

"They came about five minutes after closing. We were going about our normal procedures. I was in the back in my office totaling the daily sales. This guy I didn't know and Bill—that's my older brother—came in, and Bill asked for a pair of shoes. I said, 'Not now, Billy, I'm tied up. I can get them for you tomorrow or any other time.' The next thing I knew someone was grabbing me around the throat."

MR. DOUGLAS "SKIPPER" MCNULTY:

"Yes, sir. I can say that as a fact. Even before we went to the store he was definitely drunk and didn't seem to be acting like himself. I always thought he was pretty even tempered about things. He never gave me any grief. On the way over there, though, to the store, I mean, he got to talking about his father and his brother and that his father had screwed him over, giving the family business to his brother and sister, and had been responsible for a lot of bad things that had happened to both himself and his mother, but there was nothing he could do about it now.

"No, sir, I didn't have no driver's license. I was afraid to drive anyways. I walked on down the street and over to the Conga Room. I was there until it closed. At least I think I was. I don't remember what happened after that.

"No, sir, I don't know why Mr. Galen then came out and gave me the pair of shoes. It seemed sort of crazy to me, but I thanked him for them. These are the same shoes here, the ones I'm wearing now."

Skipper McNulty lifted his legs up from under the heavy oak table and extended them out beyond the edge to show his shoes. The shoes were highly polished. Several of the jurors exchanged looks.

The coroner, a hint of a smile leaving his face, said, "So you like those shoes?"

"Yes, Your Honor, I do."

"Mr. Firestone."

"Excuse me?"

"Mr. Firestone. I'm the county coroner. I'm not a judge."

"Yes, sir, Your Honor," McNulty said.

Barnett laughed and heard Hummer laugh.

"That'll be all," the coroner said.

Everyone stood up and began to file out from the courtroom.

Victor Galen got up heavily from the table. All three hundred pounds of him. He was using his hands on the table to steady himself. They were the biggest hands Barnett had ever seen on a man.

Barnett watched Galen talk to his attorney, receive several pats on the back, then turn and lumber out of the room.

Barnett got up and walked over to Hummer. "What happens now?"

"Nothing happens," Hummer said. "The coroner will advise to exonerate. The jury will come back in and do it. They don't call these things unless they're going to exonerate. You call in a graf, two grafs tops."

"You mean we spent four hours sitting in here for that? Can't we do more, a human-interest feature or something?"

"Guy was a drunk, a fuckup, and now he's dead," Hummer said, opening his phone. "That's the human interest? Where's the human interest?"

"Well, the way McNulty held his feet out to show off the shoes, for one thing."

Hummer laughed.

"Save it for a book," he said. "It certainly isn't news."

Then: "No, amend that to a drunk, a grandstanding fuckup, and now a corpse—dead at fat brother's giant hands after diddling himself out of family fortune."

"Maybe I will," Barnett said.

"And make mention of those hands. Once they were around the poor bastard's neck, the weight alone was enough for asphyxiation. And even if that didn't do it, once he was hit it was done. Can you imagine getting hit by one of those and then having the rest of him fall on you?"

"Of course," Barnett said, "I'll certainly use that, too."

"Sure, you will," Hummer said, putting the phone to his ear. "Always leaves an impression, your first one of these.

"Hello, Desk?" he said, then handed the phone to Barnett.

"Aren't we jumping the gun?"

"Nope. You do it. Got to get started sometime."

"What'll I say?"

"Coroner's Inquest Exonerates Shoe Store Owner," said Hummer.

"Nothing about the shoes." Barnett smiled.

"That's for your book." Hummer smiled.

"Desk . . ." Barnett said into the phone

"No, no, wait a minute," said Hummer. "Let's hold on a minute."

"They're not going to exonerate?"

"No," Hummer said, "let's think about your book. First there's the unanswered question of our pal McNulty. Is it, one, he went there with Billy, as he called him, to help kill Victor and it backfired, or two, and more likely, he went there at Victor's request to set Bill up so Victor could get rid of him once and for all, and our Mr. McNulty gets a new pair of shoes?"

"Jesus Christ," Barnett said, lowering the phone, "maybe you should write the book."

"You see," Hummer said, "if you go talk to McNulty, you might just find out he's done time for aggravated assault."

"How do you know that?"

"I've been covering this beat for thirty years, Richard. I've run across McNulty before. He's not very bright, our Mr. McNulty, but he likes to dress nicely. And then there's the other character, this Gaines character. Now who do you think it was that went in the pen with old Skipper on the same charge?"

"You're kidding!"

"Nope," Hummer said. "Not at all. You should have seen what they did to the guy they did. Hammered him in the back of the skull with a carpenter's hammer for his wallet, then tossed him into a dumpster in back of the Safeway, and remarkably, the guy crawled out and lived to tell about it. This was back in '99, and now here they are again."

"Well, with Victor it still could be self-defense," Barnett said.

"Always a possibility," Hummer said.

Barnett saw the jurors already filing back in. He lifted the phone back up to his ear, ready to speak. "Now what am I supposed to say?"

"Coroner's Inquest Exonerates Shoe Store Owner," Hummer said.

The Mary Magdalene Suite

My dear Bobby, I am sorry I could not talk with you when you called but I had a client here and was with her in a trance reading then. You should have called back later. I guess you didn't have your phone and cannot call back so easily. Call again and if you call between 8 a.m. and noon you will be able to talk with me. I hope you like the new Chopin nocturne I sent you and I trust the piano is still able to play. Tell me if it isn't and we will get help to fix it right.

I have bad news to tell you.

My daughter Mary murdered her best girlfriend three Mondays ago at midnight and now Mary has to stand trial and may go to a women's prison for life. I have a good defense attorney hired and he is going to have her plead temporary insanity, then she will go to a state mental hospital for the mentally ill for five to ten years. It is a sad story of a girl who has been on drugs for these last four years and an alcoholic for eight years before that. Mary weighs less than one hundred pounds now and has no desire to live anymore. She knows she has wasted her life and all my money for the past fourteen years. I'm broke now. I have gone through two hundred and fifty-four thousand dollars in that time, trying to make something of her, but she didn't want to be anything, and has been my enemy.

So now the preliminary comes up August 15 and we shall soon see what they decide to do with her after much psychiatric evaluation with three psychs. This is the angelic-looking little girl you used to jiggle on your knee. I saw this tragedy all coming a long time ago and warned her to quit that girl. Mary is a lesbian and this was a sordid type of affair with a cheap whore girl. Mary got tired of her but the girl wouldn't let go of her and asked Mary to kill her rather than ever leave her. Mary obliged and shot her four times.

I haven't been hardly able to play at all since this happened on the ninth of this month. I did manage to finish the "Etude in D Minor" I subtitled "The Warlock," meaning male witch. It is in Gould's style. You will like playing it and I will send you a new copy of it as soon as I have my little copyist run off some copies for me. I have three more piano solos to write yet and then all I have heard from the piano spirit is completed, and I will make a piano album of twenty piano works. Then I shall go on writing another symphonic suite I have written around Mary's life story, entitled "The Mary Magdalene Suite." It is beautiful. It tells of her birth, her school days, her ballet lessons, her tragic life of drugs and booze, her loves, her career as a writer, and now her final incarceration. It is so gorgeous in melodic line you wouldn't be able to keep from crying when you hear it. If I come and get you in my car someday soon, will you come over and spend one day with me, dear Bobby? I need you near me now to comfort me in my time of heavy sorrow. We shall play music, and comfort one another. Call me and tell me what day you can come. Saturdays are good for me. Through the week is hard as I read people all day for my living, etc. So I shall await your call real soon now and long to visit with you again.

Handcrafted Dolls

They met in Rose Garden Park. She arrived late. Shane watched her set up her stand, a card table, a white tablecloth, and handcrafted baby dolls pulled from a cardboard box. She placed the dolls on the table and stood by them. She was a small blonde. His mother was a small blonde. She was prettier than his mother. He was selling glass-covered prints of pandas and bunnies with tiny red hearts painted on their chests. She thought they were awful. He agreed. They sold to single women. He sold lots of them. She sold nothing. As the day ended she sold her first doll for one hundred dollars. She was excited. He asked her to dinner. She suggested a Japanese restaurant. She selected what they ate. At fifteen she had joined the Venceremos Brigade, went to Cuba, and cut cane. She'd worked as a linesman for PG & E. She'd gone to UC Berkeley. She'd been a radical. She was still a radical. She was twenty-four, separated from her husband who was thirty. They'd been separated for a short time. The next day she sold two dolls, then a third. She thought it was unbelievable. He asked her to dinner again. They went to the same restaurant. He left his wallet on the counter and had to go back in to get it. The Japanese waitress said, "She's got you flipping out, doesn't she?" They made out in the parking lot. She had an unfurnished apartment on the ground floor of an old building. There was only a mattress and a blanket on the living room floor, a table with a single chair in the kitchen, a set of Calphalon pots and pans, and a phone in the empty bedroom. They made love. They did this repeatedly. She said, "I don't want to go too fast, emotionally." They drove to Point Arena on the coast. She made a picnic high in the Berkeley Hills. They could see all of Berkeley, Albany, and then Oakland to the south, and across the bay San Francisco with fog over Russian Hill. They spent every day of the next two weeks together. She'd had an abortion. Her husband had not wanted a baby. Shane loved her face, the slant of her cheekbones. In Oakland, a trio of black guys walking by his van saw her on the front seat circling him with furious kisses, and began singing a cappella: "... I'm hers, she's mine, wedding bells are gonna chime; singing do wah diddy, diddy dum, diddy do ..." grinning and waving at them when they looked out. Her face was flushed. So was his. It was wonderful, their energy spinning out across the sidewalks. He needed more prints. She went down to L.A. with him to get them. They made love in the Half Moon Motel on Sepulveda. Back in Berkeley he cut out all his other girls. He called each one and told them. She heard him do it. That night she went out for groceries. Someone came to her door. Shane got up and opened it. A square-jawed Chicano guy with a skull-tight haircut and a straight nose looked at him and said, "Who the fuck are you?" Shane said, "Yeah, so who the fuck who are you?" The guy turned around and walked away. Shane closed the door. She'd asked him not to answer the phone but hadn't said anything about answering the door. When she came back she cooked dinner. He told her about the guy. She said that was my husband, just don't answer the door. She was a wonderful cook. The cardboard box of dolls sat on the floor next to them as they ate. He stayed a week longer than he was supposed to. He had never been happier. She was a runner. He wasn't. Every morning she ran a circuit around Lake Merritt in Oakland. He ran with her and got stronger. He had to go back to the north shore of Lake Tahoe. It was July now, and the lake would be bumper-to-bumper with tourists. He would sell a lot of prints. He had to work there through August. She could sell her dolls. They could run on the high mountain golf courses cut between the trees early in the morning before anyone else was up. They would see deer, and the air was so pure it was unbelievable. Every day you would wake up and feel it was the most wonderful day of your life. She would love it. The sky would be as blue as the lake. The lake would be shockingly cold to swim in. There was a club there that you could sauna in afterward. He had to leave early in the morning. She said she would meet him there. She would finish the wash the next day and bring him up the rest of his clean clothes when she came.

That night when he started in again she put her hand on herself and said, "No, it wants to be quiet for a while." They lay there for a moment, and then she said, "No, it doesn't want to be quiet anymore." A week later her car loaded with all her belongings showed up at Tahoe. It parked on the lakeside of the highway with the sparkling blue of the lake behind it. He watched her walk across the dusty lot, coming along the other arts and crafts stands, and knew she was the loveliest thing he had ever seen. She brought him his folded jeans and clean T-shirts, then told him she was leaving, that she didn't know where she was going. He said, "What are you saying?" She said, "I don't mean to shock you, but I have to go." He was shocked, saying, "I don't understand this. Why do you have to go?" She said, "I wanted to tell you face to face." "Well, you have," he said, "but why?" "It's not you," she said. He tried to argue. Nothing worked. They started walking toward her car. Crossing the road she was careless about the traffic. A car came too close and he pulled her back, keeping her from getting hit. "At least spend the night and get a fresh start in the morning." "I can't," she said. "If I don't go now, I'll end up staying the rest of my life." "Jesus Christ," he said, "what's wrong with that?" "No," she said, "I can't." She kissed him and got in the car. Under all her clothing in back he saw the box of baby dolls, the box of pots and pans. It had been a good, deep kiss. He watched her drive away, going east toward Reno, her hand out the window fluttering good-bye. Coming back across the lot, he heard McMaster, the painter of the very large, very bad oil paintings, say, "What was that?" Shane said, "You tell me."

One month later, the summer over, he began looking for her. He looked for her in other cars. He looked for her in the street. He went to the lake in Oakland and watched the runners. He went to the Japanese restaurant. No one had seen her. He drove to her empty apartment in Berkeley and looked up the landlord and asked for her forwarding address. There wasn't one. He called the phone company and got new listings in every major city in the country. He made over seventy phone calls, calling everyone with her last name at least once. He called the gas company saying he was her husband, saying there was a mix-up, and had she given them their correct forwarding address? They gave him one. It was somewhere in the mountains in back of Santa Cruz down on the coast. He drove there and found the house in the redwoods. No one was inside. The doors were locked. He went around the back and opened a window and went in. It was her sister's house. He found a letter to the sister with a return address in Portland, Oregon.

A week later he spent all of his money to fly to Portland.

He checked into a nice downtown hotel. It had begun to rain. She might be living with someone. It was dark out when he found her address. Her car was parked on the street. It was her car. There was nothing inside it. The building was a three-story brick building in a block of apartments. The outside locking panel had only a numbered security pad. The famous Portland rain was now coming down. Upstairs on the third floor a lit-up window was partially open. He shouted her name. He shouted again. She looked out the window, staring down at him for a moment before she recognized him. Then she came downstairs and opened the door and brought him upstairs. Inside the door he kissed her. She stepped back and let him in. The apartment was just like the one in Berkeley, completely empty save for a blanket and pillow and mattress on the floor, and a book lying open facedown next to the mattress. A small lamp next to the book was the only light in the room. The book was *One Hundred Years of Solitude* by Gabriel García Márquez. "You're soaked," she said. "Let me dry your hair." Getting a towel, she began drying his hair. "I'm impressed," she said, "with how you found me." He didn't see the cardboard box of dolls. She went in the kitchen and turned on the lights and made some tea. Her pots and pans were hanging on hooks above the stove. She was running a restaurant in downtown Portland. She had walked in and told them how she could improve their business and just like that they hired her. The restaurant was doing well. They really liked her. "Why Portland?" Shane said. "This is where I ran out of money," she said. "I wanted to see if I could survive in a place where I knew no one. It's something I always wanted to do." "That's amazing," he said. "Is there anyone else?" He sat there looking at her. No, she wasn't seeing anyone. Something made him hesitate. She said she had to get up early in the morning. She said, "You're welcome to sleep here." Feeling it was best not to press her—she had left him, she was the one who had to come forward—he said, "I think I'm going to go. I'll get up really early, and meet you for breakfast." He told her he had gotten a hotel room. He stood and put his coat back on. He told her the name of the hotel. They set the time. She again said he could stay. He said, "No, I don't think so," trying to take charge when in fact he knew he really wasn't, but that didn't matter; it showed her he could be. She was the one who had left. She was the one who had to choose. He could be patient. He could wait. She said, "Should I call a taxi?" He told her no, he wanted to walk. They kissed again, and he left, happy with himself, knowing if it were to happen it would happen in the right way. The "right way," he thought, going outside. It needed to happen in his space, on his turf, not hers. Looking up in the rain he saw her light go out.

Walking downtown in the dark, he didn't mind getting soaked.

Early in the morning she came to his hotel and up to his room. When she came in he thought it would happen now, but there wasn't enough time, she was pressed for time, and they went downstairs and ate in the dining room. She told him to go back to L.A. and write her. He said, "No, I want you to come with me." "I want you to write me," she said, and she said it again. He got angry. She said he was too vain. She had seen him looking at the two of them in the mirrored wall of the elevator on the way down when he was thinking they looked good together. She thought he was looking at himself. He explained. She said, "No, it's because I'm good-looking and you're good-looking and you think my being with you makes you even more good-looking." He said, "That's bullshit," then said, "I don't get it. Last night you said I could stay." She said, "That's because I'm weak, not because you're ready for what I want." "I am ready," he said. "No," she said. "I want you to go back to L.A. and write me." He didn't say anything. "I know you're mad," she said, "I expect you to be." "I'm not," he answered, but he was. He paid the check and walked her out to her car and they didn't kiss and she left for work. The rain had stopped, and he flew back to L.A.

Nine months later he saw her again.

He was working in Rose Garden Park again. She wasn't. She was looking. She came by his stand with the same Chicano guy who had knocked on the door. The guy had the same skull-tight haircut and a mustache now and looked subdued and stood a few feet behind her and didn't look at Shane. She was in a dress. He had never seen her in a dress.

She was very beautiful and very pregnant.

She stepped away from the guy and came close to Shane, "I really would like to talk to you, but I can't right now. Maybe I can come by later."

For the next two days of the fair he kept looking for her. He never saw her. He had no idea where she lived. Looking for her would be pointless. When the fair was over, and he packed up his van and drove off from the empty park, he was the last vendor to leave.

Looking back all he saw was the long sweep of lawn, the packed-dirt path across it, the trees beyond the park, the big houses beyond the trees, and a small boy riding a bicycle way up at the top of the long, diagonal path.

Shane had a long, dull drive to L.A. He didn't feel like doing it. He stopped the van and parked and walked back across the street. The trees and houses at the edge of the park formed a natural bowl. The light was leaving the sky, melting the houses and trees and park into the dark.

He went out on the lawn and lay down on the grass.

The sound of the bicycle on the long path came toward him, the spokes of the bike making a whirring rill—a playing card attached between the spokes snapping against the wires as they turned—that increased and then faded as the boy went by.

Shane lay there. The mornings had been cool, the afternoons warm, the evenings cool again. The sound from the bicycle was gone. The grass was cool and damp. The work season was over with. He heard the crickets start up. He lay there for a while longer, his eyes open, and saw the small orb of soft light that was Venus appear in the dark. He opened his hands and felt the coolness of the grass. A slow wind began flowing across the lawn. Several cars, their headlights on, went by along the street. The wind was warm. The night grew quiet. He saw other stars appear. He sketched their lines—Orion, Polaris, Cassiopeia, the Big Dipper—across the dark. There was an order out there. He realized he'd never had a chance.

Together Again

" I hope you don't blow up at this. I don't think you will because now there are no more secrets between us. Trying to make it alone can really set you apart. I found myself turning from the things that really make me happy because I had no one to share things with. So I tried to overcome these feelings of gloom and depression by stopping being alone all the time and by starting to share my time with someone. Things went along okay, not great, but okay. I started feeling better somewhat, to a certain extent. But things didn't turn out exactly right. You know who I'm talking about. You saw him that one time and didn't like him. You were right. We were always arguing because of silly little incidents, him wanting me to be something I'm not. He was talking about marriage, and so on, trying to pin me down, which just made me pull away more, made him more insane, and just forced me back down into myself, which was what I was trying to get away from in the first place, which won't happen. We just don't fit. So I am sick at the whole scene. He doesn't want to turn loose, but I'm getting over him. Whatever he wants I don't care. I don't know what I'm going to plan next, or what you want to do. When and if you work out your romantic involvement with that little girl, or girls, and you feel that you seriously want to be with me, then that will be the time for us to come together to try to build again what we know we could really have with each other."

Emeralds

S itting on the suitcase on the curb outside the Intercontinental Hotel in downtown Bogotá, dripping with sweat, air temperature sixty-four degrees out, Chris thought, Well, God is either with you or he isn't. Look at this as just a test. Until you gave Zack those tickets, the whole thing was done on trust. He didn't owe you a penny until then. As soon as you bought them he owed you the twenty-five hundred back, Tori's twenty-five hundred. He will either come through or he won't. He wouldn't send you into a situation knowing it was different than he represented. He's always been honorable as long as you've known him. Break it down. One thousand for the four men on the horses; then one thousand each for them not to look in the jars they had to deliver to Zuniga; then one thousand to the lawyer in Medellín whose secretary won't release the eighty-four thousand without you making the call. Then, when you called Tori, what did you tell her? This would be the one and only time? That after this it was done? That was what the money was for? That we would both make lots of money? And this *is* the only time. And then you said, "They *are* crazy. All they do is smoke crack, get wired, and chase cunt. When I saw them in New York, and Zack just walked in and handed me the ninety thousand and walked out, saying only, 'Okay, it's up to you now,' I knew they were crazy. And then they were so fucked up they were trying to open doors that weren't even doors to their rooms." Then her saying, "I can't believe you did this. I hope this goes okay for you, but even if it does I don't think I'll be here." The unbelievable coldness in that. And then the scummy emerald dealer coming in the room here, saying, "Okay, go out and shop around. Look at everything and see how much your five hundred dollars will get you, even with any of the wholesalers. You will not get better than these." And now you've got what, a suitcase full of dirty clothes, your passport, and nothing else? No, you've still got your five hundred. Your thoughts are all over the place. Just chill the fuck out. If you go back now, you'll be short the six thousand, no, the fifty-five hundred. How'll you explain that . . . ?

An old 1984 blue-and-yellow Mercedes taxi pulled up and Alberto Ramon Zuniga got out and Chris slowly stood up, conscious of the sweat on his face.

He wiped his face.

"Amigo," Alberto said, "are you all right?"

"I'm fine."

"What are you doing out here?"

"Just getting some air."

"With your suitcase?" Alberto laughed. "I don't think so."

He grinned at Chris and started walking to the back of the car. The light-skinned driver was out and lifting the trunk lid. Chris walked over and watched. The driver pulled out six wide, thin boxes the size of rock 'n' roll posters and stacked them up against the rear fender. Cars were noisily hustling by, choking the air with oil and gasoline fumes.

Chris wiped his face with his hand. It came away sweaty.

"You want to help me with a couple of these?" Alberto said.

He looked at Chris's face and smiled.

"Mr. Chris," he said, "there are at least four or five billion people on the planet right now, none of them any more important than any other unless they decide to be. The only thing that makes any one of us any different is that decision. The decision you have to make."

"Give me a break," Chris said.

"Just help me carry these upstairs. You still have the room, correct?"

"Yes."

"Good," Alberto said. He paid the driver, and then a bellboy came out and he directed him to put the boxes and Chris's suitcase on a luggage trolley, and the three of them went inside and upstairs to Chris's room.

The bellboy laid the boxes on the already made-up bed. Alberto tipped him. The bellboy left.

"Sit down, amigo," Alberto said.

He went to the first box and lifted off the lid. He removed a colorful hand-embroidered, woven thread painting of a Caribbean seascape with sailboats, displaying it for Chris.

"That's it?" Chris said.

"That's it."

"Where's the cocaine?"

Alberto laughed. Dressed in a gray Armani suit, a perfectly starched white dress shirt, a blue Armani tie with small irregular red ellipsoids, a dark blue cashmere scarf, and an $18,458 Hublot mocha-colored watch on his left wrist, he turned the painting, displaying the narrow edge.

"It's here," he said, "pressed in a sheet between the fabric and the canvas backing."

"How do I know it's there?"

"I'll open one, but if I do there might be a problem when they come off the plane."

"How is that?"

"The dogs might be able to smell it then."

"So I'm just supposed to trust you."

Alberto grinned and let the painting fall back onto the bed, opening his arms and palms out in the air.

"Do you realize the situation you're in?"

"We're both in," Chris said. It was true. As long as he didn't make the phone call to the lawyer the eighty-four thousand wouldn't be released.

Chris realized he'd stopped sweating. Maybe it was just the air-conditioning. Maybe he still had some control.

"Let me ask you a question," said Alberto. "You went to a university?"

"I did."

"Where?"

"University of Washington."

"That's in Seattle, Washington, yes? I, myself, went to Cornell, and have a degree in chemical engineering, so we're both two fairly intelligent men. Would you say that's true?"

"Right now I don't know about me," Chris said.

Alberto laughed.

"That just proves you are. And what did you tell me earlier, that that eighty-four thousand you now owe us was borrowed from sources in New York who wanted one hundred and twenty thousand by the end of the week, or one hundred and eighty thousand by the end of the following week?"

"Correct."

"So if you don't go through with this you are now thirty-six thousand short, plus you have to try to take *that* money back into the States with you by what, stuffing it down your socks?"

Chris didn't say anything. Suddenly it felt hot to him again.

Alberto snapped open his phone.

"Who are you calling?"

"An art supply store."

"For what purpose?"

"For six Art Voyager portfolio cases," Alberto said, then into the phone: "Hey, Ramon, it's me. We need six cases."

He paused.

"Yes, the twenty-four by thirty-six by three-inch ones." This was said in Spanish.

He listened again.

"Room eight thirty-three." This also was spoken in Spanish. Then to Chris: "Do you agree?"

Chris nodded. It was the issue of trust. He hoped to Christ Zack knew what he was doing. It was entirely clear that he, Chris, was just the tool, at everyone's mercy. He had no leverage. He didn't even have enough money of his own to buy even one emerald. He had thought for five hundred he could have gotten at least one good one. That had been shot to hell. The only thing the dealer had shown him was chips. Chips that could have been green bits of glass for all he knew.

"Here," Alberto said, handing over his phone. "Call the attorney. Then I'll call downstairs and take care of the bill."

Three hours later, having made the call to the attorney's secretary, Chris got out of another Mercedes at El Dorado International and, struggling with the six art cases, took them to the Delta ticket counter, bought a one-way ticket for himself for the midafternoon flight to Bonaire, a Dutch island in the Caribbean, and checked the cases aboard, watching them being lifted one by one by the pleasant black girl in the Delta uniform and placed on the black conveyer belt and whisked out of sight.

Sitting at a table looking out over the runways and the sunlit mountains just beyond under the smooth blue Colombian sky, Chris wondered why they hadn't been taken to the x-ray machine, but then wasn't it better that they hadn't been? It certainly was.

He looked at his watch.

The flight was scheduled to leave in thirty-five minutes..

At security the screening line was short, with white-helmeted soldiers with short machine guns clipped to shoulder straps standing at port arms along the sides, and Chris reached the gate while people were still boarding.

He sat down in one of the cushioned chairs facing the doorway and watched as the thirty-five or so people going to Bonaire went through the doorway, and then heard his name being paged over the loudspeaker, asking him to please report to the gate for immediate boarding.

He got up and walked away down the concourse, hearing his name being called several additional times.

He went into the men's and washed his face and hands, combed his hair, went into a stall, and sat down and waited.

When he was certain the flight had left he went back out and ran down the concourse, looking out the long windows, seeing a silver airliner with the bright blue-and-red-tipped Delta tail airborne and heading out over the mountains.

When he reached the gate counter he slowed and asked the same Delta girl, "Was that the flight to Bonaire that just left?"

"It is," she said. "Are you Christopher Fredericks?"

"I am. I was supposed to be on that flight."

"You didn't hear yourself being paged?"

"No, I didn't. What time is the next flight?"

"Just a minute," she said. She picked up a phone, turning her back to him, the cord curling over her blue-coated shoulder, and said something he couldn't hear.

"Is there another flight this afternoon?" he said.

She raised her free hand, meaning just a minute, then hung up the phone and said, "We'll see what we can do. Would you have a seat, please?"

Chris walked off and sat down. At least the plane was gone. And so were the paintings. That part of it was no longer his problem. He had done what he was supposed to do. Zack would be in Bonaire to get the paintings out of the baggage area. In the old days you needed the ticket stubs for that. Thank God that had been done away with. All he had to do now was sit and wait until she told him when the next flight was, thank her profusely, then go back out to the ticket area and buy the next direct flight to Miami.

"Mr. Fredericks?" someone said.

Chris turned and saw a very short, dark-skinned Colombian in a blue business suit, tie, white shirt, and polished black shoes leading two policemen walking toward him.

"Mr. Fredericks?" the short man said again, looking right at Chris as he stood up. "Did you just miss your flight?"

"I did," Chris said.

"Would you come with us, please?"

"Come where?"

"Just come with us, please."

The two policemen, machine guns strapped over their shoulders, moved forward and each took one of Chris's arms.

"What is this?" Chris said, completely panicked now. Had they scanned the paintings before putting them on the plane?

"What are you doing?" he said.

"Your luggage was checked on the plane, wasn't it," the short man said, "and you didn't get on the plane?"

There were beads of sweat on the dark skin of the man's upper lip. He had a white handkerchief and was dabbing them off.

"Obviously," Chris said. "I fell asleep before they boarded. I'm not used to the time change."

Then they were walking him fast down the concourse and they came to a steel door and the short man swiped a plastic card through the security lock and the door opened and they entered and hustled him down the steel stairs, their footsteps clanging loudly in the concrete shaft as they descended to ground level. Chris asked again what were they doing as the little man opened an outside door, didn't answer him, and led the way to another exterior door which he again opened and the four of them went in this door and down a corridor and into an office and through it into a concrete-walled room with a single bed and a sink and toilet and told Chris to sit down on the bed.

"What is this?" Chris said.

"We need to keep you here until we know the plane has safely landed."

"Why?"

"We don't know what you put aboard the plane. We do know you didn't get on it."

"You can't do this," Chris said.

"Please," the little man said. "If there is no problem, there will be no problem. We'll get you on the next flight and reimburse you for your trouble. Please bear with us. This is a matter of the utmost gravity. We have received a phone call that an explosive device has been placed aboard your flight, an anonymous phone call. It is our responsibility to treat this matter with the utmost seriousness."

"You think I put a bomb aboard?" Chris said. "Who would do such a thing?"

"We don't know yet. Perhaps FARC, perhaps no one."

"That's crazy," Chris said.

"Please," the short man said again. "If you would like something to eat or drink just let us know."

The two policemen went out first, then the man.

Jesus Christ, Chris thought. What if someone *did* put a bomb aboard? I'll be so fucked! As if you already aren't. What the hell was FARC? A revolutionary group?

He looked at the dull red door with the small eye-level window, not even thinking to try it. Where would he go? Where *could* he go? The U.S. embassy? Explain that he was here to buy emeralds and found out he didn't have enough money? That he had put on an airliner six paintings filled with cocaine that were to be taken off by a different American in Bonaire, and then flown on into Puerto Rico, and next to be taken on to Miami in the morning?

There's got to be a way out of this, Chris thought.

He couldn't think of one.

He lay down on the bed, put the pillow under the side of his face, and immediately fell asleep.

An hour later the short, dark-skinned man and the taller of the two policemen came back and looked in through the thickly glassed circular window at the sleeping American.

They opened the door and went in.

"Look at that," the policeman said in Spanish. "Like a baby. Not a care in the world."

The short man laughed.

"No," he said in Spanish, "in my experience when someone goes to sleep right after they've been arrested, it means they are guilty. The innocent ones stay awake. They are nervous, agitated, and angry. Not this man. This man is guilty of something, but of what?"

"Perhaps of the stupidity of missing his flight."

"Certainly that," the short man said.

"At least if there is a bomb it will explode out over the sea and not over the city," the policeman said.

"Yes, that is true," the short man said, who gently shook Chris's shoulder now, and watched his face as he opened his eyes.

"What is it?" Chris said.

"Your flight has landed safely in Bonaire. You are free to go."

"I am?" Chris said. Then quickly said, "Thank God! Great! What about my luggage?"

"It will be held for you."

"Great," Chris said again. "That's just great."

"Thank you very much," Chris found himself saying, offering his hand. Why are you doing that? he thought. You should be indignant, not relieved.

The dark-skinned man took the hand and squeezed it with his own.

"We've got you on tomorrow's early flight," he said, "and we've booked you a room in the Intercontinental Hotel. This courtesy is ours. We apologize for the inconvenience. Let me give you my card, should you have any questions."

He handed Chris a card that read: Hector Gomez Signorelli, Lt., Policía Nacional, Bogotá, with two phone numbers, one his personal cell phone number.

Upstairs, Chris shook Gomez's hand again and said he understood perfectly, "You are only doing your job," and that as a traveler he appreciated the concern for the safety of others that the police, by necessity, were forced to undertake.

They shook hands one more time, Chris looking down at the little man, seeing something in those eyes he particularly didn't like. Then Gomez turned and walked off, swiped his card again, and vanished into another unmarked door.

Outside, Chris took a taxi, and after leaving the airport had it stop at the first mercado he saw with a payphone box. Calling Zack, Chris immediately heard Zack cheerfully say, "Everything all right?"

"That's what I want to know."

"Everything's fine, my man," Zack said. "Just get on a wee-hop to Miami and we'll see you there. Listen, we're changing hotels. We'll either be at the Raleigh or the Delano. I don't know yet. You'll catch us at either one. And we're gonna party, dude, you know that."

Back at the airport Chris used his Visa card and took the 6:00 p.m. American Airlines flight to Miami. It was a direct flight, and going through customs back into the u.s. was a pleasure, not a hassle.

It was nearly 2:00 a.m. when Chris found Zack and Kevin and Ronald at the rooftop spa and bar of the Delano, drinking shooters of tequila and snorting thin lines of the uncut cocaine off the glass tabletop.

"Well," Zack said, "no shit, here comes the gunslinger, looking for his pay. Sit down, big boy. Have a line. You won't believe this quality. It's unbelievable. Lifts your skullcap right off . . ."

"No, thanks," Chris said. "Just my money."

"As promised." Zack laughed. He looked very happy. "Plus what I owe you for fronting us the airline tickets, right? Here . . ."

He bent down and pulled a student's backpack from under the table.

"You pay the hitters back yet?" Chris said.

"One hundred and twenty gs—every bill of it," Zack said. "You just missed them."

"No. I think I saw them coming out of the elevator in the lobby. A tall one and a short one, both with short hair."

"Yeah, a tall one and a short one, both with greaseball mustaches and short hair."

"Yeah, I saw them. That's who you sold the load to?"

"No."

"Can I ask who?"

"No," Zack said, unzipping the backpack now next to the coke. "I'm cool with that."

"You can have it either in cash or in powder. Up to you. If you take powder, you'll make double."

"But I'll have to sell it."

"That's right," Ronald said.

"I don't sell drugs."

"Give him the money," Ronald said.

Zack slid the pack over to Kevin and said, "Count out twenty-five, plus twenty-five hundred small for the tickets."

"Twenty-seven five then," Kevin said.

"Twenty-seven five," Zack said.

"Plus another two hundred for the extra night in Bogotá," Chris said.

"Sure," Zack said, bending down to snort another tiny line. Rising back up, a finger to a nostril, he said, "Boy, is this stuff righteous or is it righteous? How was Bogotá?"

"Scary," Chris said.

Zack laughed. "I'll bet. You get any emeralds?"

"No," Chris said. "That whole crap about emeralds is bogus. You have to have money to buy emeralds—real money."

"Well, you got it now. You ready to do this again?"

"You know what?" Chris said, reaching out and taking the stacks of hundreds that Kevin was sliding across to him, putting them inside his jacket pocket, "I am. When?"

"I'll call you," Zack said. "Have a drink."

"No, that's all right," Chris said, standing up. "Give me a week. Then call whenever."

He bumped fists with Zack, then walked off along the bar, not looking at anyone, heading toward the elevators.

"Cool dude," Kevin said, he and Ronald watching him go.

"He is," Zack said.

Not looking back, Chris reached the elevators. He could still hear them talking, but not what they were saying.

He didn't care what they were saying.

He stepped inside, pushing the down button. As the doors closed, he took Lieutenant Gomez's card out of his wallet, looked at it as the elevator started its descent, then tore the card in half, letting it drop on the floor, thinking, Fuck him. He's got nothing on you. You've got enough money now to get some real emeralds, money you can legally make just like you planned. And now you'll make even more money, your deal with Tori can be finessed; it'll be a lot easier with all that cash sitting out on the table in front of her, no way will she leave, but if she does, the hell with that, too. Worse things can happen. There are a lot of other women out there. Besides, she's not going to leave. Not now, she won't.

The elevator slowed and stopped.

The doors opened.

Chris looked down at the torn card on the floor.

The doors started to close.

He shoved his hand between them, popping them open again.

He stepped out into the lobby and started across the floor, the warm Miami air blowing in from off the sea, thinking, Or maybe I'll stay in Miami a few more days, see what's what. Maybe that's what I'll do. Why the hell not?

Christopher Fredericks felt pretty damn good.

"He was really handsome and had an IQ of about two. He was five years older, and we were on our way to get married and he started talking about what he wanted and he wanted a toy bulldog and fresh vegetables on the table every night and I said, 'Turn the car around. I'm not going to be cooking every night, and I don't like bulldogs. I don't want a bulldog!' I was a junior in high school then.

"Then when I was forty and out at the Elks Club, Evan walked over and said, 'I'm going to marry you.'

"I was sitting with Warren and he had just proposed. He said, 'You got that wrong, fella. She's marrying me.'

"'No, she's not,' Evan said.

"I said, 'Listen, I'm not marrying anyone, all right?'

"Then Evan got my address at work from my girlfriend and sent me flowers every day for two weeks. And I had never seen him before.

"We had forty-five years together. He still visits me. Sometimes he comes in the night and sits on the edge of the bed and asks how I'm doing. The other night there was a big storm and terns were circling in the wind and Evan came in and said, 'Look, there are birds everywhere,' and I sat up and looked out the window and there was a big moon and I saw them and I said, 'I see them,' and he was standing up, getting ready to go, and I said, 'Why can't I go with you?' And he said, 'Not yet, dear girl, it isn't time yet, but I'll be here to take you when it is, and we'll be together, just like always.'

"I wish it was now.

"I'm awfully tired now."

You Promise Me

"Darling, Darling," she said, "I have never, ever come like that, I promise you!" "You promise me?" He laughed. "God, I love you," he said. Then, "Man, that just slipped out. Jesus Christ!" And she laughed, saying, "Yes, I love you, too," and they were off the bed now and standing up and dressing and quickly happy and he said, not thinking what he was saying, "We should get married," and she laughed, her cheeks flushed, completely beautiful in her French leather coat, looking at him, eyes brightly blue with those tiny flecks of yellow and green in them, saying, "Yes," the real person she was completely there then, and, going out into the hall, he said, "Was that a yes? It was, wasn't it?" and not waiting for an answer, said, "Listen, I want to do this correctly, formally," and said, "Will you marry me?" and she said, "Yes, yes, I will."

SECOND MONTH:

She'd left the table, was in lying across the bed. "What is it?" he asked. It was simple. Things had changed. How had they changed? It was difficult to explain. "Try." She turned to him. "There's something I'm now feeling," she said, "and I don't know how to explain it." "I'll listen," he said. "I know you will," she said. "I love that about you." They lay close to one another. "You're always so good to be with. I always want to be with you. That is something that is true." "Well, what is it?" he asked. "I don't know," she said, "I don't think I feel it anymore. It's gone. I don't feel it. Isn't that good?" They went back out to the others, listened to the music. Things were fine again. Everyone was happy. It was a nice party, a nice night. The next morning she said she loved him very much, that he should always understand that, ". . . but for myself it's becoming clearer and clearer that I need to live for myself for a while, only a short while, that we will still be lovers, I still want your baby, I still won't use any birth control, that I only hope more than anything that you can understand this, and will support me in this . . ."

THIRD MONTH:

She found a small cottage for herself in the Avenues in Venice. It was a block and a half off the beach and classically English. There were plants in ceramic pots and hardwood floors without rugs. The walls were eggshell white. There was a single blue couch opposite a small fireplace, and a large bedroom with a queen-size bed with a white, down-filled duvet and white, down-filled pillows. There were no pictures and no books. There was a narrow kitchen with a green tile sink and a window over the sink that looked out into the alley. There was a terrible parking place for her small BMW alongside the back fence. It was almost impossible to park the car without protruding into the alley. If it protruded into the alley it meant a parking ticket. That was her problem. His problem was he found himself always over there, hanging around even when she wasn't there, which was most of the time, and when reluctantly she finally said, "Okay," he'd said, "No," he didn't want it that way, this after an afternoon where he'd waited around for her to return from a photo shoot, and when she came in and had said what he wanted her to say, had himself wanted to say, "You know what? This is fucked, and I'm fucked, but I'm just going to steel myself against it, and truly never want to see you again, and will never see you again, I promise you," but he hadn't. Instead, staring at her as she looked at him, he doubled up on his love, trying to lay it out right into her. She just looked at him, and he felt nothing coming from her—there was only the immediate memory of the weakness of that "Okay," and he nodded and turned and went outside and got in his car and left.

L.A. is not like New York where you bump into the people you know. In L.A. you never see anyone unless you contact them in advance. It is especially rare to run into someone on the opposite side of town. Justin happened to see her in the Rose Café. He was shocked. He was parking his car outside the café. She was sitting inside by the end window. He walked over to the window. She didn't see him. She was drinking a latte. He never knew her to drink coffee. She spread a spoonful of honey on a scone. He went in and sat down across from her at a table. She didn't look up. Her hair was parted now along the left side, cut shorter on the right, swinging from the left in a long flow that was now a natural light brown, no longer blond, around the back of the graceful length of her neck. Her head was bent, the sharply cut swollenness of the pouting upper lip, the classically rounded curve of chin arching smoothly and tightly up behind the tiny ear half-hidden under the long twist of hair, those large blue eyes studying the script on the table before her, all of her even more lovely than he remembered. She never looked up. She didn't know him. He was a complete stranger. There was no past, no future. He said, "So this is how it ends." She looked over. There wasn't a flicker of recognition. "What?" she said. "Oh, excuse me, there's someone I must talk to," and she got up and left.

FOURTEENTH MONTH:

Justin heard she'd spent her savings on paying for a nose and chin job for some male model who was trying to become an actor. Justin drove by the cottage several times, always noting the little BMW parked in the alley. Several times he drove by and didn't see it there. Several times more he drove by and absolutely didn't see it there. No one he knew had heard anything about her. She had gone somewhere and made a bad movie, one friend said, but that's all he knew. "No, I don't know the name of the movie. Whatever happened to her? She was so incredible looking."

TWO YEARS LATER:

Justin heard a famous rock guitarist had bought her a house and was living with her somewhere in Brentwood Canyon and had gotten her pregnant, and then one evening some guy came over to visit the guitarist and she had gotten up from the dinner table and had walked outside with this man and said to him, "You're the most incredible man I have ever met. I have never met a man like you. I have to be with you, and I mean it, I mean it all the way," and he said, "But you're pregnant," and she said, "If that's a problem, I'll take care of it." She took care of it and went off with this man. Justin didn't try to imagine what those conversations had been like, the last ones between her and the guitarist, although he thought the same things that had been said to him would have been said again, maybe not the same things, but for the same end. Jesus, stop it, he thought. Then he softened, remembering it hadn't been that easy on her, when she had moved out on him she had left with a fever blister on her lip.

THE REST OF HIS LIFE:

Justin never heard about her again. There were times when he wondered what had happened to her. Often it was when he saw the guitarist on YouTube or heard he was doing a concert somewhere or saw his picture or read about him online in *Rolling Stone*. Once he took an old picture out that he had of her, the only one he had. She was in a one-piece bathing suit. The suit was a light blue, tight on her body, and there was nothing remarkable about her. She looked like any girl. Her figure was average. She was blonde and standing more on her left leg than her right. That was the only thing familiar about her.

FIFTEEN YEARS LATER:

He saw her again. She was buying something in Whole Foods. It *was* her. She stood at the checkout waiting behind someone. The beauty had hardened. All the softness was gone from her skin. The mouth was smaller and tighter. Her eyes were unmoving. He moved off before she could see him. He felt she had, but it didn't matter. He walked down an aisle to the produce section and picked out some apples, what he had come in to do. He was unsettled. That had been hard. When he brought them back to the counter she was gone, as he knew she would be. As he sat in the car in the parking garage he remembered running with her. Once he'd told her she was perfect, and she had blushed, turning her head, taking the kiss on her neck, on the slope of her shoulders, saying, "Drown me in compliments, do, make me feel perfect." Every morning they went on a run. They were very fit. They were running fast. It was a four-mile run. They ran this every morning. They made love every night. She always climaxed when he did. They always climaxed together. She would get very wet. Everything was really easy. The nights were perfect. They were running fast, crossing Ocean Boulevard, running along the trees and park benches on the cliff above the ocean. The path split. He went one way. She went another. His pace was really fast. She could always keep up. He didn't look back. He didn't care where she was. It didn't matter. He was breathing easily. He increased the pace. Then she was next to him, her arms going around his neck, running with him. "You," he'd said.

"Why didn't you look back for me?" she said.

"Why should I?" he'd said, putting a finger to her cheek, "I always know where you are."

"You," she said, "you're my magnet."

Darlene

She wanted a bond, not a ring. No, she didn't want to be married. She refused to be married. If you weren't married you couldn't be divorced. Either you loved one another, or you didn't. If you did, you naturally wanted to be with one another, and so you would be. She knew where they should live. That's where they would live. There was no point arguing. He didn't want to argue. She would open her legs as widely as possible, pressing her ankles into the grip of his fists, everything straight and direct, climaxing fast, saying, "That's a baby. I know that's a baby." Michael would talk to her. She liked him talking to her. She would answer, saying, "My mind is in your mind. Your mind is in my mind. Can you feel it? I can feel it." Again her belly would come up to his and start bucking. She'd say, "Now you come, baby." He'd say, "I already did." She'd pretend to be angry, and they would start all over again.

Asphalt Cowboys

"For sure she's doing what you think she's doing. Of course you feel bad. How many times you called now without an answer? Seven? Eight? She's outta town, too, isn't she, just like you? You wanna keep calling on that stupid phone? What'd she say she was doing, going for drinks after the interview? And that she needed to extend for one more day? And what time is it now? One thirty? How many hours is that? That's what goes on, man. She *is* doing what you think she's doing. Of course she hasn't called. She's not gonna call. She's not even thinking about you. She doesn't even want to think about you. You are not even on her mind. No way. Not now. That's why you'll never hear me say nothing to no one. Not now. Not never. Hey, don't get me wrong. I've done it, man, I have. I've done it in spades. My third wife, you know that Johnny Cash line, 'We got married in a fever, hotter than a pepper sprout?' That was her, amigo, my third wife. She was fine. So fine, slim little waist, big little rump, loved to hump, couldn't get enough. We were in the Marina Del Rey once, the guy on the front desk had to call and tell us to tone it down, her screams were rattling the people in the next room. All of it was good, man, all of it, until I told her I loved her, I mean truly, truly loved her, that she had me completely, not what she wanted to hear. It lasted about three years before I caught her in bed with some fat slob of a mortgage broker whose big fuckin' dream was to one day run Bank of America, Maybe, he tells her, maybe if he had the right woman with him he coulda done it, maybe he could still do it, 'n' they could travel the world together, that's what he tells her. My fine little woman, right? Jesus, fuck! Never again, man. Never! Never tell 'em shit! Like this one guy I know, owns a paving company just like me, he goes over to his ex-wife's in Newport to borrow some money offa her, her new husband's got lots of money, he's in the fiberglass boat business, and she gets him in the bedroom and shows him her new fake tits, and he says, 'Yeah, they look nice, but so did your old ones, what was wrong with them?' And she gets close to him and says, 'Don't you want to touch them?' And he goes, 'Well,' and one thing leads to another, and he starts to pull her pants down, but she says 'No,' she can't do that, not in her new husband's house, but she'll blow him if he wants. Well, he wants, 'cause, like he tells her, 'How come you always refused me BJs when we were married?' 'Because I always knew you wanted them,' she says, 'but now you're reluctant.' So she blows him, 'n' then he drives home with a boner still going on, 'cause he's still thinking about it, see, 'n' his wife comes out the front door and says, 'What are you doing sitting out there in the car? It's hot out there.' Well, what he's doing is waiting for his dick to go down, so he says, 'Thinking.' And she says, 'Well, stop thinking, and come inside, and I'll get you some dinner.' So he goes in walking sideways, like he's got something in his shoe, so she won't see the come stain that's leaked out on his pants, and then eats her dinner and feels like shit about himself on both ends, but just keeps his mouth shut to see how it'll all turn out. He's a grownup, see. Now that's why I like staying in hotels. 'Cause what you do in here, once you do it, it's done, and when you leave it, it stays in here, 'cause you know what it all boils down to? Jus' keeping your mouth shut. That's what hotels are for. You come in and order anything you want. They bring it to you. You have it. It's done. It's over. You don't tell anybody. Don't even worry about it. That's where your old lady is, isn't she? Staying in some big hotel? Keeping her dignity by keeping her distance? If my friend hadn't let his ex know he wanted blowjobs he woulda got 'em, right? And the way he handled his new wife he probably got another one that night. That's the only way it gets done, unless you want to keep sittin' in here bawling like a baby over what you think she's doing, or has already done, and, by the sound of it, is going to do again. Just assume she is doing what you think she's doing, and assume you are not going to hear anything about it, 'cause you won't. Certainly not the truth of it. She's a full-grown woman, ain't she? An adult? Just like you, right? Aren't you done with this bullshit yet? There's only one reason your phone isn't ringing and you know it as well as I do. C'mon, let's go down to the bar and get a drink. I'm buyin'. No sense in keeping this shit up. All the cryin' in the world has never brought one woman back, and that's a stone-cold fact. Time 'n' alcohol's the only thing that'll fix this thing up. That, and we'll get another girl up here. This one just for you, even better than the one I just had. It's amazing how much better you'll feel after you do that. When you get back in town and walk in that door of yours you won't have to ask no questions, you won't wanna ask no questions, and you won't have to give no answers either. Everything'll be fine. You'll see.

"C'mon, let's go. Get up. Take that damn pillow off your face, and let's go."

Your Call Is Important to Us

"Mom?"

"Hello?"

"Mom, it's me."

"Who?"

"Celeste."

"Who?"

"Your daughter, Celeste."

"Leslie? I don't know any Leslie."

"Mom! It's me! Celeste, your daughter!"

The phone goes dead.

Celeste redials.

The phone rings and rings and rings.

The message prompt comes on.

"Hello, your call is important to us. Please leave a message after the tone."

Celeste hangs up. She redials. The same result occurs. She redials again with the same result. She waits twenty minutes, then calls again.

The phone on the other end is picked up.

"Hello."

"Hello, Mom."

"Who's this?"

"Hello, Mom," Celeste says louder.

"I can't hear you."

"It's Celeste!"

"Oh, Celeste. How's the family?"

Celeste is afraid of this. This is the third time she has heard her mother say this. Celeste has no family. Her mother is her only family.

"They're fine, Mom."

"Is John with you?"

"John? Yes, Mom, he is."

John is Celeste's brother who died two months ago in August after a double heart attack while on vacation with his wife. The first attack was in a Boise, Idaho, hotel room. The second, occurring almost immediately following the installation of a pacemaker, was in the Boise hospital. Barely surviving this attack, while being prepped for the necessary second surgery, he said, "I can't go on with this. I can't do this," and passed away.

"Tell him to call me," Celeste's mom says. "I need to talk to him."

"I will, Mom."

"What did you say your name was?"

"Celeste, Mom. I'm your daughter, Celeste."

"That's right. Celeste. You are Celeste. You sound just like her."

"It *is* me, Mom."

"For heaven's sakes, I know it's you. How's the family?"

"They're all fine, Mom."

"Give them all my love."

"I will, Mom."

"You take care of them. Good-bye now."

"Bye, Mom."

"Bye."

The line goes silent.

Celeste hangs up the phone and walks over to the kitchen window and stands looking out. Yellow, gold, and russet leaves cover the backyard. They shift in the wind. The boles of the large maples are gray, the skeletal branches still holding a few of the leaves. Several more sail off and flutter down onto the others on the yellowing grass.

"Dear God," Celeste says, trying to think about anything but this.

Get out of here, she thinks, do something, go for a walk . . .

Death

The time is November in 2013. It's an unusually warm evening out. The restaurant, rated by the *Village Voice* as serving the best Chinese food in the city, is in Midtown Manhattan East. At a corner table on the left side of the room sit two well-dressed couples sharing a variety of dishes: stir-fried lotus with ginger and scallions, sliced chicken breast with baby bok choy, spicy hot and sour cellophane noodles, braised assorted fresh mushrooms, pan seared pork dumplings in a chili-soy sauce, along with both steamed white and brown rice, and different pots of tea; oolong, jasmine, and black.

"Twenty-five thousand people a day were unloaded from the trains. They gassed twenty-five thousand people a day. He watched them arriving . . ." one of the men is saying.

The other man's father, in 1946, brought a large black-and-white photo journal back from Germany. The father had taken it from the khaki duffle along with his other trophies: the small, black rectangular collar patch with the twin white lightning bolts on it; the heavy, dull, gray-green Wehrmacht steel helmet whose sides efficiently covered the ears and back of the neck, complete with leather liner and sweat-soaked leather chinstrap, that had been selected to fit the boy's head; the heavy iron and wooden sheathed German infantry bayonet whose blade, when the boy finally saw it, had a wide grove down its black length that prevented it from sticking when being pulled from a body. The father had left the journal out on the kitchen table. The boy had looked at it, even though he'd been told not to. There were thirty or so pages. The pictures on the thick paper were grainy in appearance. Each page was covered with naked bodies in huge piles stacked in open dirt pits. The bodies were skeletal. They lay in every direction on top of each other. The heads had no hair. You couldn't tell if they were alive or dead. They looked dead, but the boy heard his father say that many of them were alive. It was something the boy couldn't understand. He heard his father talking to his mother. His mother said that couldn't be true; they have to be dead. He heard his mother saying don't let him see it. He heard his father say the stench was unbearable. The boy didn't know what the word stench meant.

The man who is talking is the grandson of an Auschwitz survivor. He had found his grandfather's diaries.

"He watched them arrive, and watched them being unloaded, both men and women and children; there were many children . . ." the man is saying.

He went on with more of it. When he finished, no one at the table said anything for several moments.

All There Is

Cutler walked up the wet concrete driveway toward the side of the house. In the past thirteen years nothing had changed. The clapboard was still painted the same sundown-tinted beige. The window frames were still green. There was the rust on the wire screen in the side door. The garbage cans were in the same place. The grass along the back was still bright, well cared for, freshly mown. The car was different. Not the black, four-door, big-block Buick Century that would have been at least twenty years old by now, but a freshly washed, silver-gray, two-year-old VW Jetta, water dripping off its fenders, sitting mute under the carport roof. A white plastic bucket with a small sponge floating in soapy water sat by the steps.

He went to the door, knocked, and a young blonde girl with short hair opened the screen door and looked out.

He asked if the Moss family still lived there. "Beverly Moss?"

The girl, still holding the door open, looked at him.

She smiled.

"No," she said. "She hasn't lived here for a number of years."

"You have any idea where she went?"

"I'm sorry, I don't."

"Okay, thanks."

"Hey," she said, "you're doing the right thing."

Cutler didn't know what she meant. He saw she was a very sweet-looking girl, a little older than he first thought, maybe twenty-one or twenty-two years old. The blond hair was natural and roughly cut. She had a pair of yellow rubber gloves on and was barefoot and wore white shorts and a faded blue T-shirt.

"How is that?"

"You find someone and you spend your life loving them. That's all there is," she said.

She smiled at him again and closed the door.

Colophon

Empty Pockets was designed at Coffee House Press,
in the historic Grain Belt Brewery's Bottling House
near downtown Minneapolis. The text is set in Caslon.

Funder Acknowledgments

Coffee House Press is an independent, nonprofit literary publisher. All of our books, including the one in your hands, are made possible through the generous support of grants and donations from corporate giving programs, state and federal support, family foundations, and many individuals that believe in the transformational power of literature. We receive major operating support from Amazon, the Bush Foundation, the McKnight Foundation, the National Endowment for the Arts—a federal agency, and Target. This activity is made possible by the voters of Minnesota through a Minnesota State Arts Board Operating Support grant, thanks to a legislative appropriation from the arts and cultural heritage fund.

Coffee House Press receives additional support from: many anonymous donors; the Alexander Family Fund; the Elmer L. & Eleanor J. Andersen Foundation; the David & Mary Anderson Family Foundation; the W. and R. Bernheimer Family Foundation; the E. Thomas Binger and Rebecca Rand Fund of the Minneapolis Foundation; the Patrick and Aimee Butler Family Foundation; the Buuck Family Foundation; the Carolyn Foundation; Dorsey & Whitney Foundation; Fredrikson & Byron, P.A.; the Jerome Foundation; the Lenfestey Family Foundation; the Mead Witter Foundation; the Nash Foundation; the Rehael Fund of the Minneapolis Foundation; the Schwab Charitable Fund; Schwegman, Lundberg & Woessner, P.A.; Penguin Group; the Private Client Reserve of US Bank; the Archie D. & Bertha H. Walker Foundation; the Wells Fargo Foundation of Minnesota, and the Woessner Freeman Family Foundation.

The Publisher's Circle of Coffee House Press

The Publisher's Circle is an exclusive group of individuals who make significant contributions to Coffee House Press's annual giving campaign. Understanding that a strong financial base is necessary for the press to meet the challenges and opportunities that arise each year, this group plays a crucial part in the success of our mission.

"Coffee House Press believes that American literature should be as diverse as America itself. Known for consistently championing authors whose work challenges cultural and aesthetic norms, we believe their books deserve space in the marketplace of ideas. Publishing literature has never been an easy business, and publishing literature that truly takes risks is a cause we believe is worthy of significant support. We ask you to join us today in helping to ensure the future of Coffee House Press."
—THE PUBLISHER'S CIRCLE MEMBERS
OF COFFEE HOUSE PRESS

PUBLISHER'S CIRCLE MEMBERS INCLUDE:
Many anonymous donors, Mr. & Mrs. Rand L. Alexander, Suzanne Allen, Patricia Beithon, Bill Berkson & Connie Lewallen, Robert and Gail Buuck, Claire Casey, Louise Copeland, Jane Dalrymple-Hollo, Mary Ebert & Paul Stembler, Chris Fischbach & Katie Dublinski, Katharine Freeman, Sally French, Jocelyn Hale & Glenn Miller, Roger Hale & Nor Hall, Jeffrey Hom, Kenneth Kahn & Susan Dicker, Kenneth Koch Literary Estate, Stephen & Isabel Keating, Allan & Cinda Kornblum, Leslie Larson Maheras, Jim & Susan Lenfestey, Sarah Lutman, Carol & Aaron Mack, George Mack, Joshua Mack, Gillian McCain, Mary & Malcolm McDermid, Sjur Midness & Briar Andresen, Peter Nelson & Jennifer Swenson, E. Thomas Binger and Rebecca Rand Fund of the Minneapolis Foundation, Jeffrey Sugerman & Sarah Schultz, Nan Swid, Patricia Tilton, Stu Wilson & Melissa Barker, Warren Woessner & Iris Freeman, and Margaret Wurtele.

For more information about the Publisher's Circle and other ways to support Coffee House Press books, authors, and activities, please visit coffeehousepress.org/support or contact us at: info@coffeehousepress.org.

LITERATURE
is not the same thing as
PUBLISHING